Novels by Annabelle Lewis

The Carrows Family Chronicles

Charlotte McGee (Book One)

Titan Takedown (Book Two) – Available Summer 2018

Charlotte McGee

BOOK ONE OF THE
CARROWS FAMILY CHRONICLES

Annabelle Lewis

PePe Press
Eden Prairie, MN

Publisher's Note:

This book is a work of fiction. People, characters, places, events, and situations are the product of the author's imagination. Some historical and celebrity names appear in the novel in order to place the story in a historic or modern cultural perspective, but these names are used in an imaginary context and do not suggest that any of the incidents ever happened.

Contact Annabelle at annabellelewisauthor@gmail.com for questions

Text Copyright © 2017 Annabelle Lewis
All rights reserved.

ISBN-13: 978-0-692-89674-7 (Paperback)
978-0-9993368-0-9 (Ebook)
First Edition

Cover Design: The Book Design House
Editor: Erin Liles
Manuscript: Annabelle Lewis
Publisher: PePe Press
Interior Designer: Manon Lavoie

Library of Congress Control Number: 2017917719

Eden Prairie, MN
Produced in the United States of America

10 9 8 7 6 5 4 3 2 1

Dedication

For Alana, my beautiful Petunia

Prologue

Charlotte was anxious about what her father had asked her to do. She did what was instructed of her, however, and left her friend Jennifer in the outdoor living room with the sliding window walls next to the pool. The room, with hand-cut stone above a fireplace, the heavy wood-beamed ceiling from which a gold chandelier hung, was often used by Charlotte as a quiet place to hang when she wanted to come inside from the gardens and pool. Detached from the house, it was a cozy yet formidable room, richly decorated with Spanish and Moroccan accents, bridging the outdoor sala and pools with the rest of the mansion, her home, Whispering Cliffs.

She and Jennifer weren't really friends, but they had a class together this their senior year in high school. The reason Jennifer Brookstone was now sitting alone in the room, the doors open to the cross breeze, was because Charlotte's father, Henry Carrows, had asked her to make it happen.

Leaving Jennifer, she'd been instructed to go back to the house on some pretense and click a walkie-talkie button, the mate of which would receive the tone sitting by the arm of her father and his companion who were seated near the outdoor living room. Charlotte did this. Her father was now alerted that Jennifer was in position and alone. Charlotte picked up a pair of sunglasses she'd purposefully left waiting for her, and looked at the time. Waiting the instructed length of five minutes, she returned to Jennifer who had obviously been eavesdropping in on her father's nearby conversation. This was the anticipated outcome.

Charlotte stopped, staring at Jennifer, who looked like she'd been caught doing something, then walked over to the doors nearest the pool and closed them. She turned around and appearing flustered said, "Maybe we should wait to go out until my dad finishes his meeting."

She grabbed Jennifer's arm gently and said, "Come on. Let's go."

Later that evening, Jennifer long gone, her mom, Julia, her dad, her sister, Carey, and she were in the kitchen.

Henry asked Charlotte, "So you're certain she was listening?"

"I think so," said Charlotte, standing with her back against a counter.

"Tell me why you think this," he said, mildly impatient yet with an instructive tone.

"She seemed nervous, scared, a little jumpy when I got back. There wasn't anything else going on in the room. There wasn't a TV on or music playing. I could hear you talking, so she had to have heard you too."

Henry nodded and got up from the table. "Thank you. Keep me informed if she says anything to you. I've got to make a call," he said and left the room.

Charlotte turned to her mother. "Do you think she's going to get in trouble? What's going to happen now?"

"Geez, Charlotte," Charlotte's fifteen-year-old sister, Carey, said, sneering and walking past her to the fridge. Opening it, she grabbed a Coke and shut the door. "Who *cares*? She's just a stupid girl from a stupid family. What do you care anyway? Gawd, don't act all fake now. It's not like she was really your friend anyway. The family will get whatever they have coming. Daddy's in charge. Just do what he says for once."

Carey left the room. Charlotte thought about that and had a terrible pang of guilt. She suddenly felt like she'd made a horrible mistake. But her dad had asked for her help, and she was supposed to help her family, wasn't she?

Julia got up to leave the room as well. Charlotte said, "Mom. Mom, do you think I did something bad? Should I have tricked Jennifer like that?"

Julia sighed. "It's what we do, Charlotte. Carey's right, your father knows what's best. It's time for you to grow up."

Charlotte was left alone in the large kitchen. She didn't know what to think, but she knew how she felt, and she didn't like it. Upbraided by Carey, dismissed by her mother, and used by her father as some pawn in his latest game, her stomach was in knots. It all felt wrong. But being a Carrows meant she was expected to participate in their schemes. They'd made that clear.

Maybe though, if she got away from them, she wouldn't have to play the part of a Carrows at all.

Chapter 1

———————

Charlotte McGee was desperate. But she was not without gifts. She needed to find a job right now, today, because her financial situation was grim. She had done a little research and had a broad idea of where to look for work. After giving her wardrobe a mindful inventory, Charlotte appointed herself with, as she referred to it, the costume of the day. Today she needed to appear extremely confident to pull off the crucial task. She wore a paneled black zipper dress with a three-quarter sleeve and a kimono style print skirt with black pumps. Her hair was slicked back and set off with a black cloche hat, Downton Abbey style, with flowers on the side. Not a traditionally modern look, but she needed to set herself apart. She knew that the hat alone would give people pause. And when they paused, she would be ready for them.

She entered the high-rise office building in Manhattan. Her research told her that there were two commercial real estate companies in the building, and she decided that she would play them off each other. Having previously gathered as much information as she could about each company and the main executives, she went first into the office of Klein Brothers. Approaching the front desk and looking purposefully lost, she addressed the receptionist in a nicely flustered fashion and asked something simple and easy.

"Hi, there. I was looking for a Mr. Jon Frank? I think he's the real estate broker for the building?"

The receptionist was now, as planned, at ease, and seemed to imagine that Charlotte was just in the wrong place, so she was willing to be helpful and chatty. Which was perfect. And expected. "Oh, he doesn't work here. He works on the twentieth floor at Frank and Son. Maybe you got that mixed up because of the family reference in the names," she said and smiled encouragingly.

"Oh, wow, I can't believe I got the names mixed up! I know both of those firms are involved in commercial real estate, right?" Volley it back, nice and easy.

"That's right. Mr. Frank is the leasing agent for this building as well as several others downtown. You could say he is our competition to some extent. Mr. Klein Sr. and Mr. Frank go way back," she shared.

"Gee, I have an interview with Mr. Frank. I don't suppose Klein Brothers is hiring too?" Charlotte smiled.

"I don't think so. I haven't heard of anything."

"Well, I better get up there right away. Thank you for your help. You have a beautiful office here."

"You're welcome. Good luck!"

Hmm, so if Klein Brother's wasn't hiring, then she'd better make it happen at the other real estate company. Charlotte headed back to the elevator and pressed twenty. She was ready. This was it. As she got off the elevator, she saw a sandwich vendor coming out of a neighboring office, and she approached him.

"Hi, there," she said with a dazzling smile. "I was wondering if you could help me? Do you ever sell lunch to Mr. Jon Frank at Frank and Son's down the hallway? Because I have an interview there in a few minutes, and I thought maybe I could treat him to lunch. If I could pay for it in advance, we wouldn't have to exchange money while we're with him. Does he have a favorite sandwich or anything he usually purchases from your cart?"

"He does. He likes the hot dogs, and he usually gets a lemonade too. Sometimes a Coke."

"Okay," she said and paid him for two lunches with a generous tip. "Thanks so much for your help. I'll just make my way over there now, and you'll be by in the next five or ten minutes?"

The kid nodded and happily tucked away the extra ten bucks. "Sounds about right. Ten minutes."

"Okay, thanks again for your help!"

Walking into the foyer of Frank and Son Realty, Charlotte took in the lovely but small foyer, empty receptionist desk, and the glass windows of an office occupied by Mr. Jon Frank. He looked busy on the phone but made eye contact with her and gave a finger indicating he would be right with her. Coming out of the office with the excitement and enthusiasm of a born salesman, he extended his hand to Charlotte. "Hello. I'm Jon Frank. Sorry, we are a little short staffed today. Can I help you?"

"Yes, but I think we can help each other. I'm looking for a job."

Visibly deflated and a little angry now that he realized she was not a customer, he responded, "Oh. Well, we're not hiring anyone right now. If you want to leave your resume or something, I'm sure we'll keep it on file and let you know if anything becomes available." He went behind the receptionist desk as if looking for something to get or write with, but he seemed to not really know what to do.

Charlotte got the sense, and her senses were rarely wrong, that he was the only one that worked there. Times might not be so good right now for Mr. Frank.

"As I said, Mr. Frank, I think we could help each other. I need a job, and you need clients."

Charlotte watched as he stopped fiddling behind the desk and really looked at her. She saw that he wasn't expecting her directness. She could also see the look of impatience on his face and the once over he gave her, eyebrow raised and head cocked as he looked at her somewhat ridiculous and purposeful hat. She put a hand on it and smiled at him, inviting him to comment.

Mr. Frank had paused. Which was the point.

"Maybe you want to take your hat off since you're inside now."

"Okay. I can do that. But I would rather discuss my proposal."

Before he could respond, the lunch vendor came through the door with the cart. Jon, no longer really interested in impressing the girl with the hat, ignored her and pulled out his wallet as he said, "Hey, Marcus, yeah, I could use one of your dogs."

Charlotte jumped in. "Marcus! Great timing! We'll take two dogs and a couple of lemonades. It's my treat, Mr. Frank."

Marcus said, "Mr. Frank, she already paid me for it out in the hallway."

Pausing again, Mr. Frank looked back at her, and while they made eye contact, she seized the moment to this time emphatically say, "I can help you."

"You may be smart," he said as he put his wallet away and accepted his lunch from Marcus.

"And I know you are too," she said and smiled, "so please just take a moment and listen to my proposal. Let me be your receptionist for two days this week. You don't have to pay me, and we'll see how it goes. After that, I'm positive you'll understand how valuable I could be to you. What have you got to lose? Also, you should know, I will be approaching Mr. Klein today with this same proposal. But I would rather work for you."

He looked at her, considering, and after swallowing a mouthful of his lunch nodded. "Okay. Two days. You look capable enough. Let's see how it goes."

The next day, Charlotte showed up in a very conservative black coat-wrap dress with three-quarter length sleeves, sporting her grandmother's Cartier diamond and gold brooch. Her nails and lips gleamed ruby-red, and her dark hair was down but parted in the center and pushed away from her face. She was hatless today but bore flowers. She placed the bouquet on her desk and asked Mr. Frank about his day, his schedule, and the clients he would be meeting. Mr. Frank told her he had only one appointment that day with Mr. Antonio Alphonse, an up and coming clothing manufacturer who might be interested in renting office space in the building.

Charlotte went back to her desk and did some research on Mr. Alphonse, his life, and his company. Around eleven o'clock, Mr. Alphonse arrived and was immediately whisked into the conference room with its skyline windows for his meeting with Mr. Frank.

While pretending to be very busy, Charlotte kept a close eye on the sales discussion and saw an uphill, tenuous negotiation playing out. Mr. Alphonse wasn't sure he wanted to become a tenant.

Charlotte wrote on a piece of paper. She then opened the doors to the conference room and handed the piece of paper to Mr. Frank. It said:

> *Say these words out loud and smile. "Now?"*
> *Smile. "Excuse me a moment." Leave me alone*
> *with him for five minutes, then knock on the*
> *window and beckon me out to the front lobby.*

Mr. Frank looked at the paper, and maybe because he was not afraid of an angle and maybe because things weren't going really well, he was intrigued, and so without missing a beat, he did as the note instructed and left.

Charlotte, alone with Mr. Alphonse, smiled, went to the window, and stood with her back to him. "What a beautiful day we're having."

She heard a polite but unenthusiastic, "Yes, it is."

She turned and smiled. "May I show you something?" She gestured out the window.

Politely, Mr. Alphonse came over to the window and looked out. As the two of them looked at the skyline, she asked him if there was anything out there that inspired him. Not waiting for an answer, she said, "What inspires me is looking at Ellis Island." She delicately pointed with her finger. "My grandmother arrived at Ellis Island less than sixty years ago. Imagine that. Coming here with nothing and then taking advantage of any opportunities that she could find. It's like a constant reminder to me. I look to that island when times are difficult and when I need a reminder of what is really important. The island is solid, my grandmother was ethical, and wonderful opportunities are out there. It instills confidence too, don't you think?"

Charlotte's research had told her that Mr. Alphonse's clothing business had been in the family for generations, and she knew there was a good chance his Italian ancestors had immigrated to America through Ellis Island.

"It is quite a sight."

"The resolute, determined immigrants who came through Ellis Island into America toward their dreams of success. Standing here in these beautiful towers looking over Manhattan, it's easy to forget where I started, but it's a powerful history, and it keeps me grounded."

At that moment, Mr. Frank knocked on the window and beckoned her back to the lobby. She smiled and nodded a respective goodbye to Mr. Alphonse and said, "I'm sorry for the interruption in your meeting. I hope you have a wonderful day." And she turned around and left.

"What are you doing?" Mr. Frank asked as she returned to the lobby.

"Just go with it. I softened him up, so go back in there and confidently close the deal. Say to him, 'Okay, do we have a deal? I'll take a check for the first month's rent, and my assistant Charlotte will deliver the papers to your office this afternoon.'" Mr. Frank stared at her, but again, decided to try it.

Charlotte glanced over to see Mr. Alphonse watching them. He turned from gazing out the window and looked at the two sophisticated people in discussion by the beautiful flowers in the lobby.

He agreed to the deal.

As he was leaving, Charlotte said, "We are delighted you'll be a tenant here with us at the Ramsey Towers, Mr. Alphonse. Before we decide what time you'd like me to deliver the lease papers to your office, do you mind if I ask if you have any important appointments this afternoon?"

"I have a meeting with someone at 4:00."

She smiled and put her hands casually in her pockets. Cocking her head, she said, "Would you have any objections if I deliver the papers, in person, at about 4:10?" Giving him a slow, encouraging nod, she watched him consider.

"I think after four would be fine."

Charlotte arrived at Mr. Alphonse's office at 4:10 that afternoon and asked the receptionist to break into the meeting with Mr. Alphonse and his client. Charlotte explained that he was expecting her. "Will you just let him know that I'm here with the contract and would like to pop in for a quick signature?"

The receptionist wasn't sure but appeared to decide to believe that Charlotte knew what she was doing. She went into the meeting and repeated what Charlotte had told her. "May I ask her to come in?" Mr. Alphonse was hesitant too but seemed to remember their conversation and so gave his consent. Charlotte was waved in. She glided in with the envelope in one hand and her handbag in the other tied with a Hermes scarf, à la Babe Paley. She greeted Mr. Alphonse.

"I'm so sorry to interrupt, but I was told to deliver the documents to you in person. Would you sign for them, please? It will just take a moment." She placed the documents in front of Mr. Alphonse and made sure the client saw the letterhead of Ramsey Towers on the envelope. As he signed the paper, she said, "Mr. Frank asked if you would meet him at the Morrell Club this afternoon at five o'clock?"

Mr. Alphonse glanced briefly into Charlotte's eyes, as she gave him a captivating smile and blinked slowly, communicating her intent. He looked quickly at his watch and his client, and said that would be fine. Charlotte gave the client a charming smile, apologized for the interruption, and left.

Sometime later Charlotte learned that Mr. Alphonse closed his deal too.

———————

The next day Charlotte arrived at work and popped her head around the corner into Mr. Frank's office as she gently tapped on his window.

"Good morning, boss. Did you have a nice evening? Is there anything you want to discuss, maybe a performance review of my work here for you?"

He sat back and again assessed this young woman who seemed to easily captivate the people around her.

"Ah, yes. A day one critique. All right, well I'd have to say, based on *one day* of work, that it's going very well."

She gave him a coy smile, bowing her head in mock acceptance of his approval, and said, "And what does the rest of your week look like? Is your schedule quite booked with interested applicants?"

"Right now, I don't have anyone else scheduled to see the building until Thursday. Mr. Mikhailovich, an older gentleman from somewhere in England, needs an office for a publishing house he is introducing over here."

"Okay, well, let me do some research on him for you, and I'll let you know how I think you should play it."

"I'd be very grateful," he said mockingly and went back to his work.

Later that day, she told Mr. Frank that he needed to acquire a tea service for the meeting. "Victorian, silver, and be sure to have some beautiful teacups." Mr. Frank frowned at her and the idea, but she pursued. "Really, Mr. Frank, I think you'll be making a smart investment, and I believe it will help you close this deal.

"I'll be back on Thursday morning to prepare the tea. But that will be my third day with you, and that was not our arrangement. Are you prepared to make me an offer if you close the deal on Thursday?"

"Yes, I believe I will." He gave her a cautious smile. "What kind of *deal* do you have in mind?"

Charlotte didn't say.

On Thursday, Charlotte arrived dressed for an English tea. She wore a pastel yellow and white color-blocked chiffon midi dress with cap sleeves, cinched at the waist, with pearls, bright pink lipstick, and her hair pulled back in a low bun. She used the beautiful tea service set and steeped some tea she brought with her. Very shortly thereafter, she pleasantly greeted Mr. Mikhailovich near her flowered reception area and kept an eye on the visit.

And, of course, in due time, she entered the meeting and brought Mr. Frank a note that said:

> *Give me five minutes alone with him and then knock on the window to beckon me back to the lobby. Say to him now, "Excuse me for a moment," then look at your watch.*

Mr. Frank did as instructed. He was a little fascinated and curious about what was going to happen.

After Mr. Frank left the room, Charlotte looked at the slightly confused and annoyed Mr. Mikhailovich and said, "Would you like some tea?" Charlotte knew he'd already declined the tea offer from Mr. Frank, presumably because he thought it was too fussy a set up for two men. She didn't wait for him to answer but began pouring a steaming cup of the mild tea into a china cup and placed a lemon slice, spoon, and napkin together while she spoke.

"You really should try this, Mr. Mikhailovich. Did you know the founder of this building had the architectural firm of Moreberry and Shute from London design the interiors of most of our larger suites? He was actually a Russian native, however, and this was his babushka's special recipe."

Charlotte smiled. He was interested. He had a babushka, but then she already knew this.

"I had the pleasure of meeting him here in this office one time, and he told me that when life got very hectic, he would stop and have a few sips of her tea to remember her strength and remember that she helped make him who he was." She indicated for him to try it with a little lemon. "I think you'll find that even just a little will be very refreshing." Mr. Frank knocked on the window. She smiled and excused herself. She had a lingering presence.

Mr. Frank and Charlotte glanced into the room, watching Mr. Mikhailovich sip his tea and gaze at the skyline. They both smiled at his back but didn't look at each other. "It appears," said Mr. Frank, "that Mr. Mikhailovich may just want to make a home here, Charlotte." He looked at her and raised an eyebrow. "Maybe you should do the same."

Chapter 2

So now Charlotte had a job. But she had known she could get one if she used the skills she'd learned growing up in a family of master manipulators. She'd been taught that if you did your research and really understood what other people wanted, and if you could figure out how to deliver it, you would be successful. If you really understood what made that person tick, you could also use it against them. A winner by any means. Her family's motto. When she used her skills and her appearance, she usually made an impression. Her wardrobe, her confidence, and her intuition had always been inspiring to others when she let them be seen. Unlike the rest of her family, who at times could be called grifters, she had always been uncomfortable using her talents to con others. But she'd tap into them now that she needed to provide for herself and her daughter, Petunia.

Charlotte got home and saw James on the steps. James, her tenant, sometimes took care of Petunia when she needed to go out. But lately, James had a way of watching Charlotte that made her uncomfortable.

Charlotte saw her nearly three-year-old daughter hiding under the stoop by the side of her townhome's garden level where James lived. She was playing hide and seek. "Hi, James! Where's Pinky?" She winked.

"Well, it's the craziest thing, Char. One minute she was here, and the next she just disappeared! She's as quick as a bunny, and you've got to get up early in the morning to catch her!"

"Don't I know it. I wonder if she could be hiding in the garden again. Petunia?" she called out. "Petunia, Veruna, Sweet Puddin Pie, come out, come out, wherever you are!"

"Mommy!!!" Pinky shouted as she jumped out in front of Charlotte.

"Sweetie Pie!" Charlotte scooped her up. "It's so good to see you. I missed you so much today," she said as she applied generous kisses to Petunia's head and face. "Muah, muah, muah, my little angel. Did you miss me too?"

"Yes, Mommy," Pinky whispered into Charlotte's hair as she held on to her tightly.

"Let's go inside and see what we should have for dinner, okay? Do you want to have spaghetti tonight? Or do you want to have witches?" *Witch* was her code name for sandwiches.

"Witches! With ears and smiley faces!"

"Witches it is. But only if you eat all your carrots, too."

"James, did you want to come up for witches or do you need to run?" said Charlotte.

"Thanks for the invite, but I've got some studying to do, and I'm all set in the witches department." He smiled.

"Okay, maybe next time. Thanks again for taking care of her. We'll see you later," Charlotte said as she walked up the stairs with Pinky in her arms.

"Bye, Jamie," Petunia said over her mother's shoulder.

That night Charlotte sat down on the bed and stared at her reflection in the large leaning floor mirror. She really wondered how she appeared to others. She'd been a successful chameleon for most of her life. Right now, she saw a young woman who had very thick, darkly auburn hair and green eyes, who was fit and toned and had been pampered with just enough products and procedures to be very pretty. She liked what she saw, but she also knew she could make herself appear basic, forgettable, and very average. From the time she was a very little girl, she'd been a master at channeling an image and changing her identity.

It comes naturally for little girls to play dress-up and have fun in costumes and makeup. But in her family, Charlotte was encouraged to take the game of identity swap to any lengths she pleased. She remembered her closets filled with costumes and accessories. On any given day she could be a girl with long hair or short, a boy with short hair or dreads, an assortment of animals, fairies, ogres, dinosaurs, planets, sea creatures, and of course, Disney characters. Any manner of dress-up her vivid imagination came up with was applauded and well financed. Her parents believed her "gift" must be encouraged and playing dress-up was the first natural step.

Her family. Did Charlotte miss them? She certainly thought about them enough. Especially her Mom. Several years ago, Charlotte had moved far away from the West Coast where she was raised to become one of the many in a team of faceless masses in New York City. Or at least that was her goal. Back then. She realized now that she would never be able to cut ties with them in her mind. They were always there and definitely in her gene pool.

Charlotte stretched and shook off some of the memories. She threw herself onto the treadmill in front of the TV. This was a nightly ritual. Even though her family encouraged her imagination, they above all else encouraged discipline. Once again, she was in lock step with her stronger-than-hell gene pool and worked with that discipline each and every day.

She told herself that discipline was a good thing and that ritual could be calming and relaxing. It had nothing to do with how she was raised. Since Pinky was asleep in the next room, she didn't want to put on her headphones and listen to music in case her little girl woke up. Instead, she turned on the TV for some more ritual relaxation.

Charlotte loved reality shows. They were all a study of human nature. Also, they played a role in her discipline track to stay current. There was that stupid word *discipline* again. She told herself she was watching the *Real Housewives* because it was a funny diversion and pointedly showed her how the crazy side of society looked. And she loved *Project Runway* for the fashion and the enjoyment of the creative work.

After her short run, she got a glass of wine and took it with her to the tub. Another ritual to help keep her grounded. Apparently, she needed a lot of them. It felt good to soak and relax. She was happy that she now had a good job. Even though she had to use a little of the basic "connettes" as she referred to them, she was still proud of her plan. She wanted to use her entre as a receptionist and parlay that into becoming an invaluable member of a company that would then reward her with a decent commission, enabling herself and her daughter to survive in her Manhattan townhome. She wanted very badly to be respectable and to live what she considered to be an honest life, but she knew her success would have to be won by balancing the standards of what was good and decent and the moderate cesspool of grifting, which was her birthright.

Thank goodness for James. He had been a godsend to her and Pinky. Over the years she had used him on and off as Petunia's babysitter, but now that job would turn full-time. She had a great relationship with James and felt fortunate that she'd found someone she could trust, but lately, she sensed something had been off. When they met, he was a teaching assistant at NYU while she was studying as an undergraduate. They became friends, and for the last six months, he had been renting the garden level of her townhome. James was now a full-time student again, working on his dissertation, so he was around a lot more and could be flexible with hours. She wondered if it was time to tell James the truth about who she was. Maybe he already knew.

The next morning, Charlotte woke excited, ready to finally start work at a decent company in a real job. She was happy and happier still when she woke to Pinky's sweet butterfly kisses on her cheek.

"Good morning, Mama," Pinky whispered. "I am a little butterfly. I give kisses with my wings. Butterflies give kisses to the people they love the best."

Charlotte grabbed her baby, who squealed with delight as she was smothered with big mama kisses in return. "I love you, Petunia! You are such a wonderful little girl and the best present in the whole world to wake up to. Let's get going! Mommy has a new job now that starts at the same time every day, so you and I will have to get up every morning, and while I get ready for work, you'll get ready for your new school. You go brush your teeth, and I'll start breakfast."

Petunia was only too delighted to begin the day. For her, every day was a new adventure. Charlotte had just enrolled her in a new preschool by their home. It was a huge change in their lives, but if she were going to have a job, Pinky would need daycare. James could only help so much in the afternoons. It was going to be expensive, but it was a commitment she had to make if she wanted to finally start a career. She needed to make a living to support them, and now that she had finally graduated from NYU she was ready to begin. So far, Pinky had adjusted really well. She'd been happy and excited during her first two weeks at preschool, and Charlotte thought this was a good sign. Like most moms, Charlotte was happiest when her daughter was happy, which should have meant she was happy all the time.

That day, she arrived at work looking professional, smart, young, and relevant. She had on an Alexander McQueen tartan wool dress with sheer black stockings and calf-high tie-up, high-heeled black patent leather boots.

"Good morning, Charlotte! Well, thank goodness you aren't wearing that awful hat today, but a tam might go with that one... it has a very Scottish feel," said Mr. Frank, amused.

"I'll take that as a compliment. Thanks. I'm excited to be here. So, I was hoping we could spend some time today going over the tenant list and perhaps a few introductions in the building? I really want to be an asset to the entire company, and tenant relations would be a great way to start. What do you think?"

To say Ramsey Towers currently had a very small staff in its leasing office was an understatement. Mr. Frank had a larger staff when the building first opened but, unfortunately, it opened as the recession hit the market. Fortunately, the building was already filled to enough contracted capacity when the crash hit that it was mostly self-sustaining, but there was a lot of empty acreage to fill and not a lot of need for much more staff in the building. The rest of the building management was handled out of another office.

"I think that would be a good idea, but I had some other thoughts. Come into my office and let's chat."

She followed him across the beautifully well-appointed space. It was loaded with the upgrade finish options of hardwoods, moldings, and wainscoting. The furniture was a tick up from basic but was lit for atmospheric sophistication in two seating areas. There were two offices, a reception desk, and, of course, the conference room.

"So, I'm sure you know you impressed me very much last week. It was a really unexpected surprise when you showed up here looking for a job. And then, of course, you caught me off guard with your tactics during my meetings. And, ah, well, and then there were the astounding results. I wasn't sure what to think of you, and frankly, I still don't know, but we'll have some time to get to know each other better while you work here. Why don't you tell me what you think the position you will be taking requires?"

"Well, I know I would be an asset to Frank and Son and to Ramsey Towers as well. I see myself as a sort of partner in helping you secure tenancy and elevate this building's reputation in the market. I see myself earning a partial commission on any new business or the renegotiated contracts that come our way."

Charlotte could see Mr. Frank was surprised. He hadn't expected the word "partner" in any sentence relating to her.

"I see," he drew out. "Well, I'm not sure how I feel about that arrangement. I do believe you should be more than a receptionist, as you've proven already, but I'm not sure I am prepared to part with percentages of my commissions just yet," he said, mildly annoyed.

She could see that Mr. Frank didn't know what to do with her and that he didn't have a plan. So, as usual, when she saw someone who was off-balance and unsure, she stepped in to set them straight.

"Well, I could always take myself downstairs to Klein Brothers. They might make an offer that would show appreciation of my special talents. If you believe my special talents helped you to close two deals last week, then I believe going forward, I should be compensated by the partnership. I think my salary should be commission based, which would only be fair if I helped to close the deals. You made a lot of money last week on the leases for your two new tenants. I *know* I can make you more. My salary would only be a small percentage. Consider it a closing fee."

Upright now but clearly still unbalanced by the turn in the conversation, he said, "Wow. Really, Ms. McGee? I didn't know we were going to be negotiating so zealously for your position here today."

She stayed silent and watched as he wrestled with his thoughts. Hopefully, he was recalling how useful she had been to him over the previous three days and was intrigued enough to agree with her latest proposal. Men usually found her memorable, and she waited patiently while he brought her to mind.

"Okay, I'll give you a trial period. How about three months and 20 percent of my commission for any deal you help me close?"

She breathed a strictly internal sigh of relief and said, "That's a deal. But after three months, you will want to renegotiate because you'll value my profitable contributions, and I will deserve more." She stood up and stuck out her hand. "Mr. Frank."

"Please call me Jon." He shook.

Chapter 3

David Torres, Petunia's father, was unaware that he had a daughter. He was, however, very aware of the fact that he had wholly and beautifully screwed over her mother, Charlotte. David was living what anyone would consider a very comfortable life in Brazil, doing exactly what he had only dreamed he would ever want to do. Live well and live for art.

Growing up poor had taken its toll on someone who only wanted to dream, think, talk, and breathe art. David was always very creative and a bit ethereal. He was unhappy to learn that the real world was harsh and real and needy. As an only child, he watched his parents work brutal hours each and every day to survive as illegal immigrants in California. Born in the United States, he nevertheless always feared their deportation. The Torres family kept a low profile, kept their heads down, and worked hard to provide David with a better life.

As he grew up, people saw him as a young man with a sharp mind and the observations of an older soul. And he loved art. All kinds of art. Painting, pottery, jewelry, fashion, music, architecture, antiques, and carpentry, all fascinated him from an early age. He would pore over books and soak in the beauty of the various elements and nuance that each field embodied. David studied every aspect he could in his spare time and dreamed of one day being a great artist himself.

And he had talent. But possibly not great talent. He worked hard and eventually won a scholarship to an art program at NYU. Born poor and the only surviving child of Mexican immigrants, he had nevertheless done well academically. Combined with his potential talent, it was enough to give him the advantageous beginning on the footpath to his dreams.

He really enjoyed his time in college, and while the regular curriculum left him uninspired, the art classes and opportunity for trolling the endless museums, galleries, and shops in the city left him further spellbound and dreaming of his place in the world of art.

David and Charlotte had met in an art history class while attending NYU. They'd taken notice of one another. Charlotte had made sure of it.

She'd been attracted to him. Tall and lanky, he had a cute, goofy, slightly exotic look, which she found alluring. She paid close attention whenever he spoke, loving his passion for the subject, wondering what he was like outside of class. She made it a regular habit of sitting closely to him each day. Of course, this effort paid off.

"Hey." David leaned over to her, initiating their first conversation. "What did you think about that lecture? Wasn't that cool, about the dirty patch they left on the ceiling at Grand Central?"

"I know," said Charlotte, smiling beatifically. "All that nicotine from the millions of cigarettes, cigars, pipes, from all the people who traveled through. I mean, I know they left it for scientific preservation purposes, but the history is cool too."

David nodded, smiling back. "Hey, I had a thought. You have any time? You want to run over there and take a look at it? You're Charlotte, right?"

"Yeah. Charlotte McGee. So, that sounds cool. I'm done with class today." This wasn't true.

"All right, let's get out of here," he said as they climbed the risers.

"What about Jackie Kennedy?" Charlotte continued. "When she said that Americans care about their past, but for short-term gain we ignore it and tear down everything that matters. She saved that place from being torn down."

"She did. I've always wanted to go to the Oyster Bar at Grand Central. It's a bit out of my league though. Have you been there?"

"Hey!" said Charlotte with exuberance. "My aunt? She just sent me a few bucks and made me promise to use it for something impractical. How about I treat us to some oysters and wine?" She looked down at herself. "Oh, but do you think we're dressed okay to get in?"

"What? You look great. Really great. They wouldn't keep us out. Thanks for the invite."

"I'm excited. I've never been there before either. So, David, are you from New York?"

Their relationship built quickly from there.

————————

Charlotte McGee's family was a relatively small clan of world-class, inherently bred, lifelong conspirators and capitalistic schemers living happily on the Pacific Coast in California. They had been very successful in amassing billions by contriving events to capitalize on the opportunities and misfortunes of others. And, they lived under a different name than Charlotte. The Carrows family, a massively wealthy and infamous family much like the Hearsts or the Rockefellers. "Charlotte McGee," was, in her mother, Julia's words, "A ridiculous alias Charlotte concocted as a small child and refused to part with."

Charlotte remembered the day she came up with the name. At about seven years of age, she felt a shift in her awareness about the way she looked at the world and the way her family viewed it. As a child, she was happy and found the world to be a wonderful, magical place and felt very tender toward most everything and everyone in it. She was a protector. But she began to realize that her mother and father and older brother were very different from her.

As a small child, her nature let her love them unconditionally. But there came a time when she became aware that the things her family said were not kind. And something about the way they behaved troubled her. They laughed a lot, but she began to realize it was a different kind of laughter. It didn't spring from inside them like her joy did each day, it came from somewhere else. And *because* of something else.

One day she and her brother were baking in the kitchen with their father. For some reason, her mother and the staff were not at home. This was an extremely unusual event, and she was in a happy bubble, loving the day and loving the closeness of being together, just the three of them. After sitting down to the table, she decided she would play the adult and dish up the plates. She took her brother's plate and leaned over to scoop some of the food onto it. In so doing, she slipped, and the plate fell, and the food fell, and the milk fell, and then she lost her balance and fell off her chair.

As she lay on the floor, the milk came pouring off the table, splashing onto her face, which while physically shocking, was more emotionally disturbing when she heard laughter. She was shocked and embarrassed and didn't see the joke, and they were laughing and pointing and making fun of her predicament. Something felt bad. Something felt wrong. No one came to her aid, and so she fled to her room and cried. And no one came for her there either.

It was not a big childhood event, but something inside her clicked as she realized that she might be different from them, and it hurt. Growing up is never easy for anyone, and it is always interesting what events in life are memorable and important. Her milk bath was one. It was after that she renamed herself, and she watched her family more carefully, observing them. She became more aware and searched for understanding about the world around her, and she looked at her family for clues about who they might be. She found them.

Including her parents Henry and Julia, there were five of them in the family because she also had a younger sister.

Their given names were Charles, Charlotte, and Carey. Carrows. The name McGee came from an Irish folktale in which Charlotte found comfort that evening alone after her milk bath under the table. In her anger and shame, she wanted to distinguish herself apart from them. And in the Carrows household, aliases were always encouraged. If only to try on.

Her brother Charles was a troublemaker. She became convinced that when Charles woke each morning, his goal for the day was to find a new way to create trouble or turmoil, be in trouble or danger, or put others, specifically Charlotte, into the direct path of risk, hijinks, and drama. Even worse, there was a cruelty about his actions, and this was abhorrent.

And as Carey grew, she became Charles's little follower. She wanted to be just like him. They were merciless in their taunting of Charlotte, and they hunted her like a pair of raptors.

And in the Carrows household, this was not explicitly encouraged, but not discouraged either. Because they all viewed Charlotte as the weak one. The one who didn't have the stomach for tough games or combative competition and especially dark-sided manipulation. Her parents thought it was tough love when an ice bath of cold water was thrown into her face while she was sleeping. They thought it was just children playing games when Charles lay in wait under her bed at night to grab her arm when it slipped over the side, sending her screaming in terror. Or he would hide behind the curtains when she played or jump out of the closets when she opened them. They thought it was good hijinks when one day Charles was given the responsibility to look after Charlotte while they were out, and he did that by tying her to her bed and leaving her alone. As youngsters, this was all good fun.

Carey was more verbal in her tormenting of Charlotte. She thought of herself as superior to her older sister and would laugh at Charlotte's tears when she was moved by something. She would walk past Charlotte and whisper horrid things like "fat cow" and "lazy, stupid idiot" and other nasty pejoratives. She would throw pizza on Charlotte's bed and stain her precious stuffed animal companions with sauce. She would take the cap off a black marker, place it onto her favorite bear, and let it bleed ink onto its fur. This behavior, particularly the name calling, was not encouraged by the Carrows, but when it was reported, it was never believed. Charlotte's parents would typically look the other way.

"Mom, Dad, she's terrible!" Charlotte would plead with her parents for understanding. "She calls me names all the time!"

"I do not." Carey would roll her eyes when forced into another tiresome family conference, which for Carey was an opportunity to perfect her lying skills, something she would excel at as she got older.

"Charlotte," implored Henry, exhausted again with the *emotions* his oldest daughter displayed, which he time and again expressed were a weakness. "Ignore her. If she said something you didn't like, you just need to toughen up and ignore it. People say things all the time. You need to place yourself above your emotions and deal with the situation. If you continue to become a victim of your weak sensitivities, you'll never be a success. Just turn it around, sharpen up, become stronger. These tears all the time, they need to stop."

"But you're not seeing the point, Dad," Charlotte tried again. "It's wrong. It's not right that she stole my diary and read it. It's wrong that she constantly calls me names like *stupid* and *pig*, and it's wrong that you're not stopping her! It's not okay that she's mean! It's wrong that she answered my phone and told Mark that he should stop calling me because I like someone else! She's a liar! She's mean! Why won't you stop her?

"Mom!" Charlotte turned toward her mother who sat passively across the room from Carey whom Charlotte observed was enjoying another victory over her. "You've got to get involved. Tell her to stop. Do something! Why are you always letting her get away with everything?"

"Charlotte," Julia said, "just let it go. Your father's right, you're just too sensitive. You take everything so personally. And, Carey, if you really did take Charlotte's diary, you shouldn't have done that. I think we should all try a bit harder to get along."

"Mom," Charlotte said softly, tears rolling down her face, feeling horrible that once again she was not being heard and supported. "She said I'm a loser, a weirdo, and I heard her on the phone with Janel telling her about some of the private stories from my journal. She was laughing and making fun of me, and you know she and Janel are going to tell everyone about what she read. Mom, please, believe me."

"That's enough," said Henry. "We've talked about this enough. Carey, did you steal Charlotte's journal?"

"No. She's the one who's lying."

"All right then," he continued. "One of you isn't telling the truth. Charlotte, why do you think she did this?"

"Because I heard her on the phone with Janel. She could have only gotten it from my diary!"

"Carey," said Henry, exaggerating his patience. "Did you *read* Charlotte's diary?"

"Oh my god, Dad! She's making a big deal out of this, and it's nothing! I was in her room and happened to see it open and read like a few sentences. I mean, gawd, it's all too much. Why would I want to read the stuff she writes down anyway? It's boring."

"All right, Charlotte, your sister happened to glance at it. She won't do it again." He gave a hardish glare in Carey's triumphant direction and continued, "And, Charlotte, you will work on your attitude. I don't want any more tears around here. You've got to toughen up. As you can see, there are two sides to any argument. In my opinion, you're 80 percent responsible for this problem. If you weren't so overreactive and incapable of managing your emotions, we wouldn't have to deal with these constant conversations. I think you should go to your room and think about it. I don't want to see either of you in my office with another one of these disagreements again. Toughen up, Charlotte. You're a Carrows, and you'd better start acting like one."

———

The Carrows were a difficult family to love. And Charlotte wanted to love. It was her nature.

She did eventually break away. To school at NYU. Her father purchased a townhome for her, and she accepted it. It was a gift from her father, who told her that once she was finished wasting her time dreaming in school, she would have a base in the real world from which to work. She wanted to live in the dorms with the other students, but her dad didn't want too much influence to be worked on her by silly college kids who were "destined for a life of mediocrity."

Thanks, Dad.

Charlotte was happy at school in New York. But she was a bit of a loner. Partly because she lived in a spacious townhome off campus, partially because she was an observer. She held herself back. She knew she was capable of blending in, but she was equally as comfortable being quiet and taking in life one precious moment at a time. But she had always been interested in boys, and David from her art history class became more than interesting to her.

Almost immediately from their first kinda-date at the glorious Grand Central Terminal and Oyster Bar, they realized they had chemistry and began to date. For very different reasons, they were both private with their personal lives. Charlotte rarely spoke of her family and didn't typically let anyone see her "apartment" either. She was worried what conclusions they would draw from such an expensive home and knew that they would ask a lot of questions about her background, a subject she didn't share with anyone.

David was equally private, but not about his background, more so about the future he wanted for himself. He shared freely about his upbringing and parents and his struggles to get to New York, but he kept to himself his growing realization that he was sick of being poor and the dark thoughts and pressures that it brought.

"When are you going to let me see where you live?" David asked. "We only meet on campus and on dates. You know I hate my room. Darren is such a pig, the whole place smells like dirty socks. Maybe your place is nicer? And we could be alone there, right?"

Charlotte was dreading what David would think when he finally saw her townhouse. By Manhattan standards, it was large, and she knew that he had no money. If he saw her home, he would obviously have questions, and their relationship would almost certainly change.

"I don't mind a smelly roommate. Besides, Darren's nice. Why don't we hang out there? Or we could go to the MOMA again. We could do more research for your Met application?"

"Oh, come on. I don't want to hang out in that room myself, let alone with you. Let's go to your place. It would be nice to relax with you somewhere quiet and alone... where we can study." He grabbed her, putting one arm around her back and one hand behind her head, and kissed her. Deeply.

He is wonderful, she thought as he released her. There was so much passion between them. "Study? Is that what you really want?" she said with a dubious look.

He continued to hold her. Looking into her eyes, he said, "You know I want you. But we could do some studying too if you'd like. Or maybe we could take the day off and play hooky. Just you and me in your private lair? Come on, Charlotte, I don't understand your reluctance, baby. Help me out here."

"It's... it's just complicated. I don't know. I've got some privacy issues, David. I'm sorry. I know it's probably weird.

You think it's weird that we've never been to my place, and I guess it is, but I have my reasons. For now, could we just leave it and go to your place? Maybe Darren will be gone."

He stared at her, kindness in his eyes, hands on her waist. "Here's what I know. I know that I love you, and I know that I'm willing to wait. For you to trust me, I guess. I've watched you. You're a strong person, but then sometimes you seem sad, and when I ask you about it, you always change the subject. But I know something is there. Maybe something you're confused about? But you can trust me, Charlotte. Truly. I promise I'll never hurt you.

"Come 'er," he said and immersed her in his arms.

He was so understanding. David was turning into the man of her dreams.

Chapter 4

Eventually, Charlotte began to realize that if they were to have any future in their relationship, she would have to trust him. She would have to trust him completely, and that would mean being honest with him, sharing with him her background and her life. As they were walking through the park, she decided it was time to tell him about her family. She didn't know how she'd do that, but maybe she'd start by telling him her real last name.

David had his hands in his pockets and seemed to be deep in thought. He did that a lot, and she found herself wondering what he was thinking about during his silences. He was mysterious sometimes, but she liked that too.

"What are you thinking about?" she asked.

David glanced in her direction and then back to the park. "Oh, you know, just worried about my job and wondering if my boss will ever give me more responsibility. I think I've earned it. I've been working there for the last four years. I mean, I know it's been part-time with school and all, but still. I would really like to have him release the keys to the kingdom and trust me with the silver."

David had been working at the Metropolitan Museum of Art in the curatorial departments. Starting as a summer intern his freshman year, he'd worked that into a part-time position, hoping to show himself to be an asset to the many departments. In addition, he'd been giving guided tours in Spanish, hoping to earn goodwill with his bosses and build his resume.

"I'm sure they will. They've already given you access to some of the inventory in the storage areas. That's a big deal! Do you know what your plans are if you don't get offered the position in the exhibitions department? You haven't said." Charlotte was worried that if the job he was reaching for didn't come through, he would consider moving out of the city. He was so private about his intentions.

"I haven't decided. But after graduation, I'll be out of the dorms and on my own! I think I could make it if they offered me a full-time position as an assistant curator, at least if I can shack up with Darren and some of his buddies in the apartment they're looking at. God knows I love a closet." He gave a half-hearted smile.

He seemed down, and Charlotte thought it was time for him to see her place. But knowing how worried he had been only made her feel bad that she had an amazing townhouse all to herself. She knew when he found out, it would be a shock. But she realized she couldn't hide it from him any longer.

She stopped walking. "How about we finally go to my place. There's something you need to see."

David lit up. "What?" he said with a questioning look. "Your place. Really?"

She nodded. "It's time."

Happier now, he said, "So where is it anyway? Should we grab a cab?" He looked around, anxious to go.

"No, let's take the train back to campus. We can walk from there," she said, her heart beating wildly now that she'd made the decision.

And they did weave their way toward the West Village. On a quiet tree-lined street, she stopped in front of a string of townhomes and looked at him.

"David, I haven't known exactly how to tell you about my life and my past, so I've kept them really private. I'm scared of what you'll think of me now, but my *apartment* doesn't change anything. I'm sure you'll have some questions, so let's just get this over with."

His face froze as she turned and started up the steps of the building in front of them.

"What, are you saying that you live here?" He pointed and stared at the three-story brick townhouse. "Are you kidding me? Whose is this?"

"Just come up, and I'll show you." Charlotte got out her keys and gave him an apologetic look. She pushed open the beautiful teakwood front door, and they walked into the parlor level of her home. The large room was painted a bold turquoise with backlit recessed bookshelves and ornate hanging lamps. Stuffed, comfortable sofas and vintage club chairs faced a fireplace and an entertainment area with a wall-mounted TV. There was important art too. Chinoiserie-inspired porcelain vases and an antique French napoleon clock stood on the mantle under a small sketch by Degas once owned by Charlotte's grandmother.

She shut the door and turned to him. Pale and bewildered, he didn't look good. Was he angry? "David, this is my home. My father purchased it for me when I moved here from California. I'm not really close to him, but he wanted me to have a home here, so he gave this place to me as a gift. We've had some difficulties in our relationship, and I think he wanted to use this place to help mend some badly broken fences between us. I'm not sure that the bribe really worked, but I took it. And it's mine."

David, his voice quiet, his eyes wandering round the room and landing on the Degas, said, "What are you saying? This is yours? Really? You own this place?" He walked further into the room. "You mean you've lived here all this time, all the time I've known you?" He stopped, turned toward her, and stared. "What is this?"

"Okay, I know this is a shock, but please don't be mad at me. If you knew all the stories and my background, you'd understand why I kept this a secret."

"I'm not sure about anything right now. I don't understand. You said you own this place? Who is your family?"

She began to shake slightly. "David, the truth is that I was raised in a home called Whispering Cliffs, off the Pacific Coast." She stopped and took a deep breath. "And my family name is... Carrows."

She actually saw his face go ashen as he sat down on the arm of a sofa. "What are you telling me?" he said quietly. "Are you telling me that your family is the *Carrows* family? *The* Carrows family of Southern California? 'Cause I know of them, Charlotte. Everyone knows of them. They are only one of the richest families in the country for god's sake."

Charlotte's pulse was racing; she was frightened by how this was going. God, he was looking at her like she was a monster for lying to him. But there was nothing she could do.

"David! I'm sorry I kept this from you. I really, truly am. Please take a moment and just look at me! I haven't changed. I'm still your girl. I'm still Charlotte McGee, the one you fell in love with this year and the same girl who loves you. Please believe me."

David did look at her momentarily, but then his gaze swiveled toward a family picture on a table. He walked over, picked it up, and stared at it.

"Can we just sit down and talk about this for a while? I'll answer all of your questions, I promise. Or maybe we should get something to drink. Did you want to go up to the kitchen or use the little fridge and stay down here?" she said, walking toward a small bar.

"What? Up to the kitchen?" He looked around and registered the stairs in the corner, which clearly led to somewhere. "Are all three floors yours? Christ. God, is that a garden out there?" he said as he stared.

"Yes, the garden is mine, it's private. And this is the main living area, but I don't spend much time here. The kitchen and dining room are on the second floor, and the bedrooms and baths are on the top. Did you want to go up?"

Recovering himself slightly, he put the picture back on the table and said, "Sure. Let's go up and look around." He shrugged, scowling, looking somewhat disgusted.

She crossed the room and hugged him. She held him for a while and then kissed him and took his hand. "Thank you for trying to understand, David. Come on. Let's go up."

He followed her. As she gave the tour, she spoke nervously about parts of the building that she used and loved and some of the areas that she would like to change. They eventually came to her bedroom. It was large enough to contain a king-sized bed. The walls had a parsley wallpaper above a chair rail with raised panels painted to accent the wallpaper.

"And this is my room, where I spend most of my time."

He looked around, picked up and put down a few items, and mumbled, "I don't know who lives here. I know this," he said holding one of her bags, "and this," he said pointing to a sweatshirt. "But I don't know anything about who owns the rest of it." He gestured around the large room.

"Okay. I understand," she said anxiously, her hand shaking slightly as she gestured toward the bed. "Come over here. Let's sit down, okay? I want to tell you a story. It's the reason why I haven't shared everything with you, and I know that it seems deceitful because I know all of this is a part of who I am. And it *was* deceitful in a way, by omission, and I'm sorry. But maybe you'll understand better after we talk, okay?"

It was time. She had to open up and share who she was with someone she cared about. She needed to tell someone about what her life had been like and who she wanted to be. David sat on the edge of her bed.

"My real name is Charlotte Sophia Carrows, not Charlotte McGee. I made up my own last name when I was seven, and my parents let me keep it. My dad thought it might be useful. My mom thought it was silly. But my dad always wins. I have an older brother named Charles and a younger sister named Carey. I grew up with my family in that house that you have probably seen and heard about. It was a great house, and it's still where my mom and dad live. I've been back like once since I came out here for school."

She hung her head and took a deep breath. She hadn't shared any of this with anyone outside the family, ever. She looked at David and continued. "My family is different than most. I know what you're thinking, about the money, but it isn't only the money that makes them different. I mean, I know every family is unique, and I guess mine is unique too, of course, but I think what I am trying to say is that they might be really different."

David, openly fascinated now, encouraged her. "Okay, go on. I'm listening."

"It's hard to say this, but my family is a dysfunctional mess, and again, not in any traditional, classical way. They are ruthless people. They're single-minded and have always looked out for themselves first. They play games at the expense of others, to manipulate them and break them. I don't think that's normal, even for the very rich. And I've met the very rich," she said, rolling her eyes.

"So, what happened? Why haven't you seen them?" he said shaking his head.

"It's so complicated," she paused, wanting to sit next to him to reassure him, but she realized that she needed to go on. Standing in front of him, her fists balled tight with nerves, she plowed forward and tried to explain. "They were in the middle of playing some con game on this family, and I knew the daughter, and I did something they asked me to do, something I'm not proud of, and I just didn't want to be like them, and I had to get away. They didn't get why it made me uncomfortable, but it did. They said I needed to 'cool off' and 'come back to reality,' but it was more than that for me. I needed to get away from them, forever, I think. Or I thought. I don't know. I just know I was sad and confused, and I needed to find out who I really was."

She sat down next to him on the bed. He swiveled, and their eyes met. Charlotte appealed for him to understand.

"I really needed that, David. More than anything, I wanted to learn about myself without the influences of my family around me. And I couldn't do that being Charlotte Carrows. People would treat me differently. They always have. I thought that if I was just Charlotte McGee, and no one knew who I really was, then I had a chance of discovering myself."

She hung her head, distinctly concerned that he wouldn't understand.

"And so, you know the rest, David. I moved to Manhattan, and I accepted Dad's gift of this apartment, which was probably a tax write-off or a part of some settlement negotiation, and started school. And then I met you," she said as she searched his eyes again, hoping to find reassurance

"Please, David, please tell me what you are thinking?" she said as she reached a trembling hand toward him.

———————————

David was thinking. He was dreaming again. He was marveling at the absurd coincidence that had presented itself to him. And he would soon let those thoughts play out and create future scenarios that ranged from just sheer astonishment about the absurdity of the coincidence to schemes with deep and criminal leaps.

About a year before, David had an extraordinary opportunity to work on the team that brought a traveling exhibition to the Met. It was this opportunity that was currently inspiring David to pursue his application to the exhibitions department at the Met. He felt he had found a home on a grand stage when he watched and learned what went into creating an exhibition and bringing it to life.

This particular exhibition was originally from Russia, specifically called The Romanov Jewels. David's job was to work with the various departments' curators, identifying smaller items in storage at the Met that could be displayed with the full traveling exhibition. Curiosities, complementing historic pieces, paintings, silver, and other items would be additions that would come from the museum's monstrous labyrinth of storage archives. Many of the items had been in storage for years, some for a generation, just waiting for the proper use and unveiling, which would lend aesthetic value to a show.

The "Jewels" had just been on display in Dubai, and after the Met's three-month run, it would move on again. When it first arrived at the Met, it was accompanied by a representative of the exhibit who worked very closely with David and his coworkers on the transition, setup, inventory, marketing, and integrity of the original creative vision from Russia. The Met would later send a representative to the next city with the exhibition to follow the same steps. This was the job that David ultimately saw for himself. A kind of master of a small, distinguished world. A curator and knowledgeable expert on a microcosm of important art. And that would be the first of many worlds he would master.

One night, the Dubai exhibition rep, Kamal, asked David if he would join him and a few associates for dinner. David gladly accepted.

"I don't have much in the line of fancy clothes or things that would pass a dress code inspection. Where are you going?"

Kamal said, "That's all right, the guys that are in town wanted to have an Italian experience, so we're going to a place in Little Italy. It's pretty casual. What do you think? Can you make it?"

Kamal and David had been getting along well over the last few weeks, and David thought he, himself, might enjoy the evening and the thought of what he assumed would be a free meal. But more importantly, he wanted to continue to pick Kamal's brain about his experiences in the world of traveling art exhibitions.

But in retrospect, the evening, as it turned out was memorable for more reasons than David initially appreciated. Seated next to David at dinner was a Dubai native and friend of Kamal's in town for business. The man was a friend, but as David learned, he was also a wealthy patron and sponsor of the Romanov Jewels exhibit who had been influential in Dubai becoming a hosting city. The exhibit was sold and hosted in Dubai at the nontraditional Burj Al Arab Jumeirah Hotel. Overlooking the Arabian Gulf, the hotel's Romanov Jewels was a main attraction and worked to help market the hotel as a magnificent destination.

The dinner that night started pleasantly but turned into something else after the grappa was introduced. David and his new dinner companion, Victor Al Nahyan, got to know each other better.

"My new friend, I will tell you about my lifelong love of the Romanov family jewels. I find them a fascinating story, the family. The culture, not so much, but the family and the way they died and the mistreatment of them, and the misunderstanding, that is something I relate to. They were so tragic. Their life was given to them to rule by generations that ruled before them. But some of them were great, and some of them were not. And no chance, *no* chance would there be to be great if they were not raised to *be* great. And then there is that tragic boy and that terrible disease that ran through so many of the European monarchies. Yes, too private, too tragic, so stupid.

"I tell you," Victor continued, "even though they were overthrown for good reasons, mind you, I still feel compassion here." He pointed to his chest. "A family, a great historic family, a ruling monarchy for years, should *never* have been treated like that in the end. And so, I follow the history and the stories and try to support the memory. It means something to me."

David was interested in this man, interested in learning about his passionate involvement in the Romanovs, and he began to understand Victor's generous contribution.

"There was one particular piece in your curiosities addition that has me very intrigued but somewhat upset as well," said Victor, draining his glass and gesturing for more.

"Oh, which piece is that?" David said, reaching toward the bottle, obliging.

"The canary yellow diamond ring," he said, meeting David's eyes with an intense stare.

"Oh, you mean the paste replica we displayed?"

"Yes. That is the one. Ohh, the original!" Victor swooned. "It was so beautiful, and I wanted it to be mine. For my collection. Something worn by the Tsarina herself! Something I could look at and be reminded of family and destiny and tragedy and love. A part of history, in my hands." He looked at them, sadly empty.

"Yes, I understand that the original was purchased by an American in California. Were you aware of that?"

"Of course, I was aware! I followed that diamond to auction. I was hoping to purchase it, but alas, I was detoured from owning it for personal reasons. My wife," he said, smirking, "who did not want to own the ring as much as another item on auction that day," he said with a frown. "I have deep regret for that decision, but my wife, what can I say, she is my life, and I am much too soft here." He pointed to his heart. "I remember that auction. I would have bid much more for it than it sold. And, tragically, I have to live with the fact that it was sold to a man whom I do not like. In fact, I despise him." Victor's eyes went dark at this comment. He picked up the grappa in front of him and put it back.

David saw the evening turning maudlin, and while he was enjoying himself, he didn't want to spend the rest of the night nurse-maiding a drunken Arab. But that is exactly what he did. The next day, David received a note sent by special messenger.

"My dear friend, thank you for your invaluable companionship last evening. I sincerely hope our paths cross again. Please look to me if you are ever in Dubai. I would love to introduce you to my family and the grappa of the desert."

————————

The intense canary diamond had a name. The Tsarina's Fancy. A sixty-five carat, brilliant cut, fancy, vivid yellow diamond once owned, worn, and adored by the Empress Alexandra Romanov. A gift from Nicky to Alix, two happy young lovers who would rule one-sixth of the globe, on their wedding day. The Tsar Nicholas II was extremely fond of jewelry and kept a book recording each of his valuables, documenting their significance. He made drawings of hundreds of pieces, recording the significant date, occasion, or anniversary the gift was presented upon. A copy of the Tsarina's Fancy was journaled in one of his books. It was also a custom at the time to make almost identical paste replicas of some of the more memorable pieces. Peter Carl Fabergé was only too delighted to indulge their royal highnesses with whatever whimsy suited them.

A paste of the Tsarina's Fancy was one of those. During the revolution and for a few years prior, some in the aristocracy had the foresight of things to come and fled Russia. Many of the Grand Dukes and Duchesses found asylum in England and were entrusted with the safekeeping of some of the family jewels. The Tsarina's Fancy was last seen around 1916 with the empress in Tsarskoe Selo, an eight-hundred-acre compound fifteen miles south of the capital where the Romanov family escaped from the city's madness. Their principle residences were found in the one-hundred-room Alexander Palace where they would later be put under house arrest. It was believed the paste duplicate of the Fancy was given to a Grand Duchess, and the real one was hidden with her maid. Both rings ultimately survived the revolution in exile and were eventually put up for auction some years ago. The real Fancy was sold for $3,500,000, and the paste was donated to the Met. The Tsarina's Fancy was purchased by Mr. Henry Carrows.

And David knew this. He had also cataloged and replaced the fake diamond into inventory.

But that would all come to him later. For now, David was reeling in other emotions. *My god, my girlfriend is rich? She had always been rich and was hiding it from me? She's a god damned Carrows?* He didn't know how to react.

"I don't know what to say here, Charlotte," he said, getting up, ignoring her outstretched hand. "I'm just amazed. This is all a little too much to believe. I can't believe I didn't even know your real last name! Does anyone else know who you really are?"

"I don't think so. I had my name legally changed to Charlotte McGee before I moved to New York and before my name was put on the deed to this place. Everyone knows me as Charlotte McGee, and as you know, I don't show anyone where I live."

"You could have told me," he said, indignant. "You could have told me at least part of it, like in small pieces if you needed that much mystery. I don't really know who you are now, who you really are. There must be a million other things I don't know about you too. Your life, your experiences, your family. Man, I told you everything about my family. I shared all the painful stuff too," he said, his brows knit with confusion and anger.

"David, I'm sharing now. Don't you see? This is really hard, and you're so important to me, and I'm trusting you now. Please understand that."

"I understand that you're telling me now. And I'm glad you think you can trust me. But I'm gonna need some time to get my head around all of this," he said as he ran his hands through his hair, looking around, observing the items in the room. "Damn, that's why you always had so many clothes—you could afford all you wanted. And that's why when I asked you about your family you always changed the subject. And why you don't seem to have many close friends.

"I don't know, Charlotte," he said as he began to leave the room. "This is really wild."

"I love you, David. It's still just me," she said disheartened to his departing back.

———————————

David survived the disclosure. Shocked but delighted that he'd found himself in a romantic relationship with a very rich girl, he was more than happy to forgive her for her deceptions. Not long after the revelation, he moved in with her. Why wouldn't he? He loved her townhome. He had never experienced such luxury of accommodations and being surrounded by beauty in his own home environment. He loved the back garden and the full chef's kitchen and the washer and dryer and the tub! My god, to actually take a bath in a big, deep tub where he could lounge and relax in quiet surroundings. In the heart of Manhattan! And the linens and the space to move and stretch and breathe without bumping his head on something or digging through boxes or drawers or carving out a cramped space to study in the evening. It was overwhelming, but he got over it.

Charlotte was relieved that he recovered from the shock.

"I'm so happy that I can finally share my home with someone! David, isn't it great to come back to our home at the end of the day? We're like this wonderful little family now."

And he did love it there, but he still had a load of questions, which she was mostly reluctant to answer. "Tell me more about your family. What are they really like? What happened between you guys?"

And more questions like, "When was the last time you saw them? Do they come here? Have they been here since we met? Have you told them about me?"

And still more questions, digging a little deeper about her finances. "So, it must cost a lot to keep this place running well, and the taxes and stuff, right? Do you have millions in the bank too?"

Charlotte would answer some of the questions, a bit at a time, but she was still hesitant. Eventually, David pulled out of her that she was at terrible odds with her family. They didn't speak regularly. Specifically, she didn't speak at all with her sister, and with her dad on only rare occasions. But she did speak with her mom and her brother. She also shared with David that she received an allowance from her family and had some money in a trust that she would get when she turned thirty. So, while she was still technically living in a millionaire's home, her regular disposable income wouldn't set the world on fire.

David also originally assumed that her situation could easily change, and Charlotte could be super rich if she just reconciled with her family. But as the months wore on, David realized she had no intention of doing that. She seemed perfectly content to live in her big house, go to school, and play happy family with him.

He was becoming discontent.

Chapter 5

David's family and his entire life were clouded with poverty and fear. And fear of poverty. And fear of separation, because his parents had entered the US illegally. David, however, was born in the US, which automatically gave him birthright citizenship, but not, of course, his parents. They lived in perpetual fear of detention and deportation. They made sure there were always signed releases following David to each school, entrusting someone with his care if immigration officials suddenly swooped in and took them away. They made a will giving all of their possessions, moderate though they were, to David in the event something suddenly happened. And they waited. Until David turned twenty-one.

After that milestone, David could legally become his parents' sponsor and petition for them to be lawfully admitted to the US for permanent residence. But there were huge obstacles. His parents, having entered the country illegally, would have to return to Mexico as a consequence of their unlawful presence in the United

States. The unlawful time they spent in the US accrued, and they had to deal with a time bar penalty, which in their case was set for ten years. Only after that ten-year period could they *begin* the process of David's sponsorship to obtain return visas. And this pissed David off. But his mom and dad had decided it would be better to face the ten-year exile and then at least have the possibility of returning to the United States. They wanted to share their older years with David and the grandchildren they hoped for in the country that had become their home.

David's parents were currently in Mexico, no longer in the small ranch house in California they had worked their entire lives to build. And when they returned, he had no idea where they would live. He didn't know what the future would bring, but the present was filled with pressure.

But now something new had entered his life. He had a rich girlfriend. By fucking accident. He just happened to find her interesting and beautiful, and her privacy issues worked for him because he was fundamentally a private person too. And he knew she loved him. He loved her too, a little.

When he initially found out about her status, he leapt at the hope that he might ride her ample coattails into something wonderful. He might be rich too! My god! That would be perfect. But as he became more and more informed and had begun to learn the depth of her reluctance to reattach herself to her family, he became disenchanted. He couldn't understand her. He would have given anything to have access to all that money and privilege, and she could not technically be bothered with it. She didn't miss it because she was comfortable. David wanted to be more than comfortable, and he didn't believe Charlotte would ever be the vehicle to get him there.

———————

About a year after David moved into the townhome, Charlotte received a formal invitation to a party at Whispering Cliffs, her childhood home, her parents' home. She decoded the invitation for him, telling him it was basically a self-celebration centered on their generous donation to a museum they helped establish in San Francisco. She wasn't interested, but David was dying to go.

Set to happen in two weeks, he had his work cut out for him to convince her to attend. And she needed to pay for it. Because even though he had acquired the exhibitions department position at the Met he had long desired, after moving in with Charlotte, he'd become obsessed with wanting more. His current compensation and future at the Met no longer gave him comfort. He had bigger dreams.

He lay awake at night in her beautiful bedroom in a bed that felt like a giant marshmallow and wondered what life would be like if he were the master of his own universe. Lately, he had also been worrying about how to keep Charlotte from sensing his displeasure over her obsequious complacency. She had recently suggested the possibility of starting a family... without marriage. Why would he want to do that? To have children with her might be a way to gain access to some of the family money but without benefit of marriage, it might be a long shot. He hadn't even met her family. What if they hated him and never gave her an inheritance? God, what if she was so bent that she even turned it down?!

His feelings of dissatisfaction and desire for greatness steered him toward dark thoughts. He knew one thing was certain. He didn't love Charlotte the way she loved him. But that didn't really bother him. What kept him awake at night was the planning, because he remembered the stone. And that was something he could use. After they received the invitation to the party, he began to fully expedite his course of action. He had worked out a Plan with a capital *P.* But there would be a lot of unknowns he would need to address along the way.

One aspect of his dedication to the Plan was wooing Charlotte. He had to get to California. He had to convince her that it was time, with him at her side, to take the first step in healing the rift between her and her family. He used his own family and their painful separation as an emotional call to action for reconciliation with the only family she would ever have in her life. "It's just a first step, honey. It doesn't have to mean anything more than that. Just take the leap with me. I will be there for you today, tomorrow, and always."

And she finally acquiesced. Behind the scenes, the rest of the pieces were also coming together, and David was ready.

Once he convinced her to accept the invitation to the party, Charlotte was touched that David had become so attentive to her needs and so understanding of her worries. He'd been extremely doting and solicitous of her over the last couple of weeks, trying so hard to make her feel comfortable. He constantly spoke about how they could conquer anything and get through anything if they did it together. She loved him for it.

With the anticipation of their visit, they shared long conversations about her feelings and about her ancestral home. Charlotte explained to him that while the event was supposedly centered on a Carrows sponsored art show at The Cheung Gallery in San Francisco, it was probably more realistically a combination of sponsorship and something to do with stroking the ruffled feathers of the local gentry, press, or notables. It was just another day in the life for the Carrows.

Whispering Cliffs was nestled on a high bluff overlooking the Pacific Ocean and had partial ownership and controversial access straight through the Topanga State Park. Its trailheads of roughly thirty-six miles wound through open grassland, oak trees within the cliffs, and the canyons of the Santa Monica Mountains. It was a paradise, primarily for the very rich.

The home was one of a handful in the country with a name and pedigree. Purchased and developed by Hank Carrows in the 1920s, over the years it had become controversial. Occupying a coveted position on exclusive acreage, community leaders, environmentalists, and jealous neighbors often felt entitled to voice their opinions about the various uses of the property as if it were public domain.

The Carrows family were not oblivious to the noisy rabble, but they didn't really care. They felt above it the way humans sometimes feel toward lesser species. It just didn't matter to their daily or future lives. But from time to time, they felt compelled to play the game and soothe their community, patrons, supporters, and nonsupporters. This they accomplished by making Whispering Cliffs open and accessible to parties, fundraisers, and dinner parties for the local political hive and artisan communities.

———————

On the plane to LAX, Charlotte was anxious but so grateful to David for taking such tender care of her. He was her touchstone if things got out of hand. They'd made arrangements to fly in on Saturday, the day before the party. They would only be staying for one night at the house and planned to catch the red-eye out on Sunday evening.

Oddly, the length of the trip was dictated by David's schedule not Charlotte's desire for a short visit. David told her he needed to be at work on Monday for an important meeting with his team who were pulling together an arriving exhibit. This was his job, his career, and passion, and she understood that it was important for him to return to New York to be there for its arrival. Unfortunately, the length of their stay had caused her parents some irritation, but ultimately, they put it aside, just pleased that Charlotte would be returning home.

The party was scheduled for Sunday evening, and Saturday would be all about a small family reunion. On the one hand, Charlotte was dreading it, but on the other, she felt some relief that the impasse and healing with her family might actually begin. Maybe they'd all changed and could forge something positive and loving. It was a stretch, but it would be nice if it happened. The trip was something she might not have taken if it weren't for David's encouragement.

That Saturday evening, Charlotte and David arrived in Los Angeles and were met by a chauffeur her parents had sent to escort the couple to Whispering Cliffs. As they cleared the gate and drove down the long drive overflowing with oaks and sycamore trees, David gazed out the window holding Charlotte's hand and said, "What a beautiful place. I can't believe you were raised here."

Charlotte was also nostalgic, affected as well not just by the beauty of their surroundings but by the feeling a person can only have upon returning to their home after an extended time away. She gripped his hand and smiled faintly but remained silent as they wove through the trees, anticipating the reveal of her home.

The house was a breathtaking architectural wonder, a magnificent three-story palace with a blend of Mediterranean and Italian Renaissance revival architecture. It loomed ahead of them and featured a monumental exterior staircase that ascended onto a grand porch. The courtyard on either side of them was lined with ficus trees as the limousine drove past a gigantic outdoor sala and to the quietly ethereal turnaround.

"My god," David said in a hushed tone. "Charlotte, I had no idea it would be so beautiful this close up."

By now, she too was overcome with the magic of the scene, and her long absence allowed her to more closely experience the home from the eyes of someone seeing it for the first time.

Excited, she smiled and gave him a quick kiss. "Welcome to Whispering Cliffs, David."

To say the Carrows family did not love each other would be wrong. They were classically and not so classically dysfunctional, but they had history, and that history for better or worse was with each other. That Saturday evening when Charlotte and David arrived, Charles walked out onto the porch to greet them. As they got out of the limo, he walked down the grand staircase smiling from ear to ear.

He walked swiftly up to Charlotte and grabbed her, not letting go for some time and whispering, "Welcome home, Sis. It's so good to see you. I've missed you."

Holding her brother, she was immediately reminded why she loved him too. It never mattered how much he did to upset her, he had an infuriating way of making her smile in spite of it. His charm was legendary and went a long way in explaining why he was able to get away with almost anything he ever did. She'd always known that they loved each other, but they were very different from one another.

Pulling away, she gestured toward David and said, "This is David. David Torres. David, this is my brother, Charles."

Charles held out his hand and said, "Nice to meet you. Thanks for escorting my sister across the country. We're glad you're here."

David thanked him, and Charles asked the driver to bring the bags inside. "Where is everyone else?" Charlotte asked. Charles threw his arm around her shoulder as they walked up the stairs.

"Inside, waiting breathlessly for you. Ready to pounce on you like a cat," he said, his hands in claws. "For you too, David." Charles laughed and slapped David on the back. "In the salon."

Once inside, David stopped and stared heavenward toward an old-world bronze and crystal chandelier and frescoed ceiling. The three-story atrium always made new-comers stop and stare. Charlotte was amused by the response, and she watched David, his mouth hanging open, surveying the ceiling and the other valuable works of art around him.

"It's a smaller version, of course," Charlotte explained looking up with him. "A replica from the Paris Opera

House, of the original one, the one that fell. The ceiling is also a copy of Chagall's work. They're beautiful together, don't you think?"

Taking his hand, she whispered, "Come on," encouraging him to follow Charles as they continued into the home and to the salon before them.

The massive grand salon had floor-to-ceiling windows on one wall showcasing the Pacific Ocean. With its three-story draperies, a grand piano, multiple chandeliers, seating areas, walk-in fireplaces, and marbled staircases on either end, the room was fashioned after an Italian piano nobile and looked out onto the loggia, gardens, and ocean.

The rest of the family rose to greet them. Julia Carrows was the first one to embrace Charlotte. She was a beautiful woman and resembled Charlotte with her dark hair and slender physique. She wore elegantly soft, flowing rose-colored chiffon silk pants and blouse and modest jewelry. "Charlotte. Baby. I'm so glad you're finally home," she said with tears in her eyes.

Charlotte felt emotional too as she turned to her father. "Dad," she said as Henry hugged her warmly and applied several kisses to her cheek. He stood back and gently held her shoulders, gazing at her with pride. "You look just wonderful, sweetheart."

Carey, in an all-black, backless jumpsuit came last and gave her sister a short hug saying, "Hi, Charlotte. Hey, I wore all black just for you. For the prestigious visit of the prodigal, right?"

"Thanks, Carey. It's good to see you too," she said, holding herself steady and choosing not to parlay.

Carey gave her largest smile and turned toward David. "So, this is your boyfriend? Hey, there. David, right? I'm Carey, Charlotte's little sister."

David looked off-balance, and he put his hand out awkwardly. Carey looked at it, amused, and then laughed and walked over and gave him a hug. Charlotte watched the brief encounter. Her sister hadn't changed much. Always stunning, she and Charles took after their father's side of the family. Different than Charlotte in many ways, Carey had lighter skin and wore her extremely thick, very blond hair, short, in a mass of curls. She rolled out of bed looking glamourous and was an enthusiastic symbol at all times eager to display the Carrows's wealth. Large jewels hung from her ears and around her neck, making Charlotte's casual style seem almost out of place.

First introductions complete, it was for all of them an instantly familiar dynamic that clicked back into place to form one whole.

"Charlotte, David," said Julia, "let's sit down. I thought you'd be tired from the travel, so we're having dinner shortly. David," she said turning her attention to him, "I understand you're from California?"

Sitting next to Charlotte on a sofa across from Julia and Henry, David took Charlotte's hand and said, "Yes. I'm from Inglewood originally."

"Inglewood," said Julia, trailing off, contemplating the city as if it were in a foreign land.

"I grew up there."

"Mom," said Charlotte, "it's east of LAX. You know where it is."

"Oh, of course. I'm sorry, David. My geography has never been good. So, your family is nearby then. Should we invite them to the party tomorrow evening? Wouldn't that be nice? Would they like that?"

David looked surprised. He blurted out quickly, "Oh. No, I didn't tell them I was going to be in California since I knew we wouldn't have time to see them. It's such a quick trip, I didn't want them to be angry."

"But surely, they would forgive you once they saw you!" said Julia, looking around for support.

Charles gave her an adoring smile. "David, how 'bout it? Should we give them a ring? Can they break away tomorrow for our little shindig?"

Charlotte was concerned. She squeezed David's hand, knowing he was lying to them. His parents were in Mexico. She turned her head to look at him, trying to communicate a plan. She saw faint traces of panic in his eyes. She answered, "Guys, they don't have much notice here. Not everyone has a tux in the closet. I don't think it's fair to ask them here for the party, but I'm sure you mean well." She gave an intense look at Charles who, as usual, looked to be enjoying their discomfort.

Julia waved her hand in the air. "Oh, come now. They don't have to fuss. I'm sure they have something appropriate. David, you really should see them while you're here. I know I'd be hurt if my child, whom I rarely got to see, was in the neighborhood and didn't take the time to visit."

Charlotte flinched, understanding that her mom was probably referring to the last time Henry was in New York and the two of them hadn't gotten together. While both

Charlotte and Henry had been disappointed, Julia had been furious that they didn't see one another.

"Mom, really. Not for the party. You'll have guests. You'll be too busy with them to entertain the Torreses." She didn't want to show them that she was desperate to change the subject.

"Perhaps, but surely you're not going to take time away from *our* visit to travel east of LAX tomorrow. We'll hardly see you as it is."

"Why is that, Sis?" said Carey, flicking a nail. "Just arrived, leaving so soon?"

Charlotte didn't appreciate the attitude from her sister but was determined not to take the bait. "David has to be at work on Monday. He's part of an exhibits team taking the arrival of a new traveling exhibition. It's important that he be there for that. The party just happens to be on a Sunday. It's a quick visit is all. We wanted to come, but we can't stay long this time."

Putting pressure on Charlotte's hand, David added, "It's entirely my fault. I apologize, Mr. and Mrs. Carrows, that we have to eat and run, as it were, but I really do need to be there on Monday. I'm sorry for the rush."

Julia put her hand to her throat and looked at Henry, who remained silent. She forged ahead. "I see. Well, I'm sure you can understand why we were disappointed, David. Charlotte, it's just been such a long time."

"And why is that?" said Carey, eyes wide with wonder, waiting like a child for someone to help her out.

Charles threw his head back and laughed. Breaking the tension, he said, "Enough." He stood. "Let's go to the dining room. You haven't even seen Rosita and John yet. They're anxious to see you too."

Charlotte was grateful for the interruption and rose along with David. "You're right. Let's go see them."

"Excuse us," said David, slightly bowing his head toward Julia. Carey sat back and started laughing.

John and Rosita were the housekeepers but more than that, almost a part of the family. They had lived at Whispering Cliffs for as long as Charlotte could remember, and she missed them too. Along the way to the dining room, she whispered to David, "Having fun yet?"

David gave her a slightly nervous and apologetic smile, but it helped her to settle down. Walking behind Charles, the rest of the family remaining in the salon, she watched David's head swiveling, his eye catching glimpses of various works of art. "We'll have some time for exploring later," she said, glad they were on the same team.

"My god." He pointed to a portrait in the dining room as they passed. "Was that a Manet?"

"It was. It's been there for ages. My grandfather Hank bought it."

"That's incredible."

"Ask Daddy about it over dinner. He loves to talk about it. He loves to talk about all his collections. Believe me, you'll fit right in with that."

David nodded.

———————

The family assembled in the formal dining room for dinner. The long room was paneled in French walnut, wall sconces illuminated the length, and precious art was interspersed throughout. The cream ceiling was elaborately carved, the wood floor anchored by an enormous Spanish rug. Upholstered arm chairs showed seating for eighteen, one end set for dinner for the six of them. A small fire crackled in a cream marble fireplace, the Manet, prominent above.

"Have a seat, Charlotte," said Carey. "No need for you to change before dinner, right, Mom?"

Julia admonished, "Of course not. They've had a long day of travel." She gave Charlotte a supportive look. Charlotte glared at her sister, who was ignoring her, a smirk on her face.

Henry sat at the head of the table, Julia and Charles on either side. Carey sat next to Julia across from Charles, Charlotte, and David. Two quiet maids attended to the meal, seeing to their needs, while Rosita remained in the kitchen.

"David had some questions about the Manet, Dad," said Charlotte.

Henry said, "Édouard Manet. One of my father's favorites. *The Races at Longchamp.* Got the Degas in the other room. The Longchamp Racecourse in Paris. Ever been there?"

"To Paris? No, sir," said David, startled.

Henry looked uncertainly at him and then resumed eating.

"Mommy," said Carey, "don't you think David should at least invite his parents over for the day tomorrow? Aren't you dying to meet them?" she said as she picked a tiny leaf of endive from her salad with her fingers and nibbled on the end.

Julia placed her fork down. "I quite agree. David? Do you think your parents would be able to visit with us during the day? We could have a luncheon by the pool. I understand the weather will be perfect tomorrow."

"Of course it will cooperate, Mommy. You're having a party," said Carey.

David said, "I don't know. I appreciate the offer, Mrs. Carrows, I truly do. But we don't have that much time here. I think it would be a distraction. I don't want you to put yourself out."

"It's no trouble, David," said Carey grabbing her glass of wine. "Give them a call. Ask them if they can break away from their hectic schedules to see their son. At Whispering Cliffs."

Charlotte said, "I don't think we should." She was upset that this line of questioning was still on the table. She needed to shut it down so they could both stop lying. She didn't know why he hadn't just told them the truth from the beginning, but it was too late to go back and change the story. She shuddered, thinking about how a retraction at this point would go over.

A bit heated, she impressed, "Really, Mom. We're not going to invite them. Okay? This is about David and me. For the next short twenty-four hours. Can we just leave that aside? I'm sure I'll meet them someday."

Shit. She knew it was a slip as soon as it was out of her mouth. Carey pounced.

"What! You haven't met them yet either? How long have the two of you been dating?"

Charlotte moved around in her chair; she could feel David squirming beside her.

Carey said, "Wait. Do they still think you're Charlotte *McGee*? David, I'm breathless. Did you tell your parents that you were dating Charlotte McGee or Charlotte Carrows? I've got to know."

Charlotte didn't know how to get her sister to back down. David said, "I told them my girlfriend's name is Charlotte Carrows McGee. They know who she is. They know everything about her."

"When you met our dear Charlotte," said Carey, "did she introduce herself as McGee or Carrows? Really. This is fascinating."

Charlotte was reaching her limit. Everyone at the table knew it. Families read each other's emotions, and they knew they were heading for trouble. Thankfully, Charles intervened.

"Carey. It doesn't matter. Let it go. David is here. We're glad he's here and that Charlotte's home. So, leave it." He gave her a hard stare, then turned back sweetly to Charlotte.

"How's school going? Do you have any plans once you graduate?"

Charlotte searched for her mother's eye and watched as she dabbed her lips with her napkin, staring at Henry who seemed oblivious to the tension and was working on his meal. She took a breath and gave a reluctant, "I don't know yet. School's fine. I'm still enjoying it. I may continue. Maybe get my master's. I've been looking at some grad school options."

"Really?" said Julia. "You're not planning to be done with your education and take some time to see the world? I've been looking forward to you finishing with your commitments out there so we could make some plans. I was hoping that we could have an actual family vacation sometime soon. Maybe sail around the Greek Islands? A friend of mine just got back from a trip over there, and it sounded very nice."

"Daddy doesn't like to travel," said Carey, sitting back in her chair, pouting, arms crossed, a long-stemmed glass of wine in her hand.

"He'll travel occasionally," said Julia, without conviction.

Charlotte looked at her dad, still silent, almost as if he was not paying attention. She knew that was not the case. He never missed anything.

"David," said Julia, "do you enjoy sailing? Do you have sea legs?"

David choked a little midsip on his wine and put his glass down nearly upending it. Charlotte was horrified. She hadn't told her family about David's family. Nor about his poverty. She didn't think it was their business. She felt terrible that he had to answer these questions.

"I don't sail. Or I should say, I've never been sailing."

Henry's fork stopped moving, and he briefly looked in David's direction under hooded brows.

"David's an amazing painter, Mom. You should see some of his work. He has some real talent. I think you'd be really impressed."

"Really, David?" said Julia. "I'd love to see your work. Have you had a show? In New York?"

"Mom," said Charlotte, exasperated that they were still going in the wrong direction. "No. He hasn't had a show. He's been working at the Met. Going to school. He hasn't had time to focus on it, but he paints. We have a studio set up in one of the bedrooms, and he's building some inventory. We've got to find an agent, but he has lots of time." She looked at him hopefully. Worried.

He said, "She's right. I haven't had the time to focus on it, but it's a passion of mine."

"He's really good," impressed Charlotte again.

"Thanks. Time will tell. I've got my plate full at the Met right now, though. I've enjoyed employment with them for some years now, and I believe I've built a strong reputation. I know people, I think, who will help me when the time is right to make the introductions and connections I'll need to have a strong debut. Art is my life. I look forward to traveling, when I have the time, and experience firsthand the treasures out there just waiting for me. I'm really looking forward to spending some time with your amazing collections. You're all so lucky to live among so much beauty."

"Luck, you say," said Henry, everyone's head swiveling in his direction. "I suppose luck played a part in it," he considered. "But not a very large one."

———————

As soon as she could, Charlotte begged to be dismissed due to travel fatigue, and they left the group. She was told that her bedroom was prepared for them; a shared bedroom in the house with her live-in boyfriend apparently was not an issue. They retreated to it as quickly as they could.

It was nearing midnight, and Charlotte was exhausted from the emotional day. She kicked off her shoes as she entered the bedroom. "Oh my god," she said as she walked over to her suitcase and unzipped it with force. "I'm so glad to be alone. God, I've been so anxious all day, I can't tell you."

She turned around and sat on the bed watching as David walked to the balcony doors. "So, David. What do you think? How do you think it's going? Was it everything you were expecting?"

———————

What did he think? He pulled back the curtains and saw the moon's reflection on the waves, the view something out of a dream. This was little Charlotte's bedroom. She grew up here. He shook his head and turned and looked at the softness of the suite, at the feminine chintz vases scattered around, brimming with pink roses, and found it just another example of their exotic and privileged lifestyle. It didn't fatigue him.

"So, this was your room growing up? Did it always look like this?" he said, gesturing to the soft pastels and tasteful decorating that was not typical of a high school student's bedroom. The age she was when she left.

"Yes, this was my room, but it didn't look exactly like this. Mom's done some decorating. My stuff must be somewhere else. At least I hope she didn't throw my things away," she said, off-balance now and looking about with concern.

"Well, what about my family? What did you think about them?"

What did he think about the Carrows? Charlotte had been right about a number of things. Her sister Carey was a bitch. Nearly every word out of her mouth had an ulterior motive.

"They were nice. I liked them."

Charlotte gave him a look of disbelief. "Really."

He smiled. "Well, yes. For the most part. I'll give you that Carey's a little bit scary. I'm sorry to see that you two don't get along."

"Don't get along? What do you mean? You're saying that like it's a two-sided thing. She's the one that..."

David rushed over to the bed and threw himself on her, lying on top of her and pinning her arms above her head.

He kissed her gently. "I'm trying to be polite here. She's kind of a bitch, okay?" he whispered. "But, I know if I say that, it will hurt you. And I don't want to hurt you."

She calmed, smiling and kissing him. "It's okay. Thanks for that. What did you think about the rest of them?"

David released her and flopped over onto his back, staring at the ceiling. "Your mom's nice. She seemed really glad to see you. I saw her tear up when we first got here."

"I know, I saw it too."

"Charles is... I don't know. It's like he has a big secret he's keeping from everyone. I kept waiting for him to say something crazy. I caught him staring at me, just smiling, a few times. I have no idea what that was about."

"What about my dad?"

"Your dad is kind of tough to read. Captain of Industry type. He kept looking at me too, sizing me up. They all were. Even when they weren't looking at me, it felt like they were. It was a little uncomfortable sometimes. I don't think I made a very good first impression with him," he said, putting his arms up, resting his head in his hands.

She rolled over and looked at him. "I think you did fine. He is hard to read. You got that part right. But I think I can read him, and I think you impressed him. Especially when you had a chance to discuss art. I could tell he appreciated that."

He closed his eyes. "It's so beautiful here, baby. It's a jeweled palace filled with treasure. I don't know why you ever left." He opened his eyes. "I mean, I know why you left, it's just that, it's all so incredible. It's the most beautiful place I've ever seen."

"You were pretty cool about it."

"Until I had to lie to them about my family. Shit. I should have known that would come up. Sorry you had to lie for me. I just didn't want to tell them about my family at our introduction. I don't know why, I'm nervous I guess. I didn't think my poor sad story about immigrant Mexicans would be the best way to start."

"David, you don't have anything to be ashamed of, you know."

"I know. I know that. I'm not ashamed of them," he said and got off the bed, then walked over to his bag.

But that wasn't true. He was ashamed of them. Maybe not exactly of them as persons, but of their poverty. Of their circumstances. He didn't want the Carrows to have a reason to look down their noses at him. And he didn't want to serve it up at their first meeting.

"You know the truth is going to have to come out sometime, right?"

He shrugged as he dug in his bag. "I 'spose. Whatever. I'm beat. Let's just hit the hay over there on that mountain that you call a bed where you probably used to fantasize about the man of your dreams."

He turned his head, looking up, and gave her his goofy grin. She looked back with adoration, which was exactly what he needed.

Chapter 6

Sunday dawned, and David was greeted by a world filled with exotic fragrances and new experiences. He and Charlotte joined Henry and Julia by the magnificently tiled pool, surrounded by elegant and manicured gardens. The immense pool area was a world unto its own, nearly enclosed by Spanish-inspired arches with shutters and decorated with Moroccan light fixtures and a dramatic fireplace. The four of them relaxed as Rosita served them breakfast.

"Thank you, Rosita," said Henry gratefully as she poured some hollandaise onto his eggs.

"I thought I told you not to make the hollandaise, Rosita," said Julia, confused.

Before she could reply, Henry said, "I told her to ignore any suggestions you made to her about modifying my meals."

Julia looked shocked as Henry patted her hand. "Now don't get riled. It's my choice. Leave poor Rosita out of it."

Charlotte, amused, said. "Rosita, how often do they sabotage your meal plans?"

"Quite regularly. Mr. Henry wants what he wants, and Ms. Julia wants what she wants. But they are no longer the same. Your father has been texting me lists lately, menus. I don't mind, but your mother seems to."

"Rosita, I apologize for Henry's behavior. I didn't realize he'd been texting you, overriding my decisions about our meals and his diet."

Henry didn't appear to be listening as he devoured his mouth-watering meal. Coming up for air, he pointed his fork at David.

"So, you haven't had a chance to look around the place yet. Charlotte, are you going to give him a tour?"

"Maybe in a little while. Mom and I were going to look over my clothes and see if I can borrow something sparkly and special."

"Jewels. Ah," said Henry, grabbing his orange juice and taking a large swallow.

"I don't think I should be too long. Dad, maybe you and David want to get a head start after breakfast. Do you have time to show him around?"

Henry took a slice of buttered toast out of the basket in front of him and shoveled more egg and sauce onto it. "Sure. I could do that. I'd appreciate your thoughts on my collections, David. You being in the art world," he said as he waved his fork in the air for emphasis.

"I'd enjoy that, Mr. Carrows," said David.

Charlotte smiled, happy that her dad had agreed to give up some of his time for David.

"David," said Henry looking over at his plate, "what are you eating over there? Did you try the hollandaise? Rosita makes the most delicious recipe. She's a superb cook. Better than some of the fancy five-stars that we've been to."

"Thank you," said David taking the offered serving dish from Henry, who watched while he poured a dollop of the rich sauce onto his remaining eggs.

"Oh, come on now," said Henry, disapproving.

"Dad!" said Charlotte. "Don't force him to eat it."

David, however, poured more, but Henry, leaning over to inspect the process, gave him a hooded look and swung his fork in a circular motion. David poured more.

"Ah, there you have it," said Henry, satisfied. "Dig in, dig in. Tell me if I wasn't right?"

"Ridiculous," said Julia, as they all watched David eat a large helping.

"Ummmmmm," he said, smiling, his mouth closed.

"I have a large appetite for life, David," said Henry, pouring coffee from the french press, adding a long stream of heavy cream.

"My wife, my home, my children, my work, I do everything large. You have to seize what you want in this life. Go after it. Savor the victories. A meek man will never succeed. Not in my book. Hey! What is the exhibition you're working on? The one you're desperately needed for tomorrow?"

"It's the Chinese art of the Qin and Han Dynasties. It's—"

"Ah," said Henry, cutting him off. "I suppose those terracotta army warriors will be a part of it?"

"Yes, as a matter of fact—"

Henry cut him off again. "Then you'll have a lot to discuss with our guest of honor tonight, Mr. John Cheung. We've been very good to the John Cheung Gallery. Gave them a huge grant to develop a new wing. Of course, our name will be on it as benefactors, but John does good work. I can count on him to make us proud over there. Not like some of the other crap that's out there. You know what I mean?" he said, emphatically pointing at David.

"You don't go in for all that modern art, like all those 'artistes' out there using different parts of their bodies to paint with, or body fluids? I even heard about one guy who used ninety cans of his own excrement to do something god awful with. You don't go in for all that, do you, David?"

"No, sir. I'd say I'm more of a traditionalist, more of a—"

"'Cause if you were," he said, picking up his napkin and wiping his mouth vigorously then throwing it on the table, "I'd say you had a screw loose. Let's get going then," he announced and stood up. "David, you're ready?"

Henry didn't wait for a response but kissed Julia on the top of the head and walked off. David jumped up to follow. "Thank you for breakfast, Mrs. Carrows, it was delicious. The hollandaise was—"

Henry yelled back to the group, "You coming or not?"

David bowed to Julia and said to Charlotte, "I gotta go. See you later?"

Charlotte laughed. "I'll find you. Have fun!"

———————————

Julia and Charlotte watched them go. Julia shook her head. "Your father is eating too much. I'm worried about him."

"He looks good, Mom," she said, uncertain.

She nodded. "He does. It's all that energy he has. At least he's been exercising. I don't know..."

"Well, what do you think about David?" said Charlotte, sitting back.

Julia took a sip of her coffee. "Ummm. He's very polite. He has excellent manners."

"Is that all?"

"I don't know, yet. I've just met him. He's very attentive to your father. I'm sure he'll enjoy our collections. He seems really interested in his art."

"Well, do you like him?"

Julia placed her cup on the table. "What's important is that you like him, honey. And what's important to me is that he's good to you and that he's brought you home. That, I like about him," she said good-naturedly.

Charlotte considered before saying, "I really do love him, Mom. I see a future for us. You wouldn't believe how sweet he is to me. He's always thinking about my needs and checking in to see if I'm okay. Especially over the last couple of weeks. He's been good for me," she said, testing the waters, not only for her mother but for herself.

"I see. I'm glad to hear you have someone you can count on out there. Have you two discussed your future? Are there any plans?"

"No. Yes. Maybe, I don't know. We're taking it slow. We love each other, that's what's important right now. I'm hoping maybe after I graduate, we could make it something more permanent. He hasn't really asked me, you know." She shrugged. "I guess I'm waiting for that."

"He'd be a fool not to want to marry you."

Charlotte looked toward the breezeway where she had last seen him. "He's no fool, Mom. I know that for sure."

"Well then," she said happily, "I wouldn't worry about anything. As long as he makes you happy. Now let's go up and see what you've brought for tonight and have some fun accessorizing it."

David was thrilled by the tour. Henry seemed to be enjoying it too, but he was taking him around the place at a clip. David could spend a lifetime devouring the background, the histories, discovering the journey the pieces had taken to arrive at Whispering Cliffs. David could spend hours gazing at them, appreciating not only the pieces on the walls, but the sculptures, the artifacts, the tasteful design elements, and the architecture of the place. Everything fascinated him.

Each vista was arranged with exquisite taste and attention to detail, perfectly situated to reflect the right balance of light, color, symmetry, and scale. Every corner they turned offered something new. David was wholly impressed. He proved himself to be an eager student and an educated and thoughtful contributor. He wanted to impress Mr. Carrows, but it was difficult.

They were in an interior sala somewhere in the house. The room had Cantera stone columns and Cantera stone floors and sixteen-foot ceilings with wood beams that beautifully anchored the room. The brushed pale-yellow walls and stone fireplace, the wood laid in ready, the delicate chandelier in the center, it was another room that had a life of its own.

"Over here," Henry was saying. "This one we call The Prince. Tell me the name of the artist, David."

Henry had been quizzing him rather than telling him the names of the artists. David approached the work and shook his head. "I don't understand, sir. I thought the Duke of Westminster owned this. Isn't that Diego Rodríguez de Silva Velázquez's work?"

"It is," Henry chuckled. "Painted in 1636. Not many people know their provenance like you do, David. I'll give you that. I'm not going to tell you how the lad came to be hanging at Whispering Cliffs though. That's for another day. Maybe..."

David didn't know how much longer he had with Henry. He said, "I understand that you purchased some of the Romanov jewelry? I had the privilege to be a part of curating the Met's archives for the Romanov Jewel exhibition and came across the paste of the Tsarina's Fancy, which we put into a display. Your name was mentioned as the owner of the original."

"Yes, that piece is really wonderful. I'm so glad we were able to bring it home. Would you like to see it?"

"Of course! Wow. That would be amazing. I spent so much time with the replica, I'd be really interested in how the real one looks and feels."

Henry led him out of the room and down a breezeway with what looked like an ancient stone wall on one side. Passing several other living spaces and closed doors, they came to a large wooden door that opened to a more modern looking space.

"This is my office," said Henry as he walked through, the walls lined with bookshelves, antique copper pieces, and art. He stopped in front of a Moroccan looking cabinet and keyed a code into a side panel that blended into the woodwork. As the doors opened, the lights came on and illuminated a display of several amazing and beautiful objects d'art, including the Empress of Russia, Alexandra Romanov's beloved ring, the Tsarina's Fancy.

Henry removed the ring from the cabinet. "The Tsarina's Fancy. It's a beautiful piece. Maybe I can convince Julia to wear it tonight. She's only worn it a few times. She worries too much about what other people think of her."

He handed the ring to David. Light caught the numerous facets, and it sparkled in every direction. "Oh my," said David, admiring the brilliant cut sixty-five carat ring.

"How does it compare to the replica?" said Henry.

"Not quite the same thing, sir. The light catches this one like there are rays of sunlight inside."

"Yes, it does, doesn't it?" said Henry, putting out his hand and then replacing the ring in the case. They looked at some of the other items, but David's mind was a blank. He tried to show interest, but it was difficult.

When they were finished, Henry closed the door, which then sealed tightly and locked.

David spent the rest of the afternoon with Charlotte, further exploring and relaxing by the pool. The activity in the house increased as it came closer to the party. Caterers, musicians, and florists arrived as well as a masseuse for Carey. She didn't offer to share.

That evening, Charlotte and David were a beautiful couple and for all the world looked happy, vibrant, and in love. She wore a fun and girly black tulle and chiffon skirt with an exquisite beaded top belted with a satin bow. Her mother had loaned her some stunning jade and diamond earrings, which enhanced her green eyes and the deepness of her dark hair. David had rented a white tuxedo jacket with black trousers in New York in preparation for the dress code Charlotte felt would be appropriate.

The house was candlelit, and the doors of the piano nobile were opened up looking out onto the sweeping Pacific Ocean. The bougainvillea trees of purple and red were lit and highlighted as torches illuminated the huge lawn and the beach below. A refreshing breeze drifted through, and piano music softly played in the background of the grand salon while an orchestra played in a small band shell outside.

David and Charlotte walked together outside, stopping to mingle with a few people along the way. The guest list included reporters from the *Palisadian-Post* and the *LA Times*, their photographers arriving early to take photos of the scene before the event. They were then sequestered to a designated area, which had a backdrop supporting the event. The guests who chose to have their pictures taken would go to them. Among the attendees were friends of the family, local politicians, artists from the San Francisco and Los Angeles areas, and some faces Charlotte recognized from her days at high school. Still in town and still making the social rounds.

Walking toward the bar, David suddenly stopped.

"Wait. Charlotte. Who is that over there by the bar talking to Charles? Oh, my god, is that Bill Murray?"

Charlotte followed his eyes. "It sure looks like him. As a matter of fact, Charles told me once that they'd golfed together."

"Oh, man. Holy shit. You've got to be kidding me. Wait, who is that?"

As Charlotte turned to look, he grabbed her and said a frantic, "Don't make it obvious. The guy, by the band shell?"

"Can I turn to see, or should we just walk over there?" she said, amused.

"We can't just walk over there. Okay, let's just keep walking, and then you can look."

"It is my house, you know, David. I am allowed to go anywhere I choose."

"I know that," he said, off-balance.

"It looks like Christopher Walken."

"Oh, man! That's what I thought. What the heck? Who else is going to be here?" he said, astonished.

"I don't know. I guess we'll just have to wait and see." She smiled, watching him try to collect himself. "Mom didn't share the guest list with me. Other than John Cheung, the guest of honor, I don't have a clue."

She laughed. "Honey, you need to relax. You seem so tense. Are you okay?" She rubbed her hand over his arm and watched as his eyes shifted focus around the grounds.

"No. Yeah. Of course. I'm okay. It's just that I've never seen a celebrity in person before. It's kinda bizarre, isn't it?" He scrunched up his shoulders.

She shrugged. "It can be. I've met a few, and it depends. I think everyone here tonight will be approachable. For all its size, it's an intimate group. Mom said a couple of hundred people, but with the space outside and the house, it will feel smaller."

"So, the house is just open for the guests to walk around?"

"Yes. Usually. There's extra security around." She nodded her head toward a large man in a suit. "But they're just here for emergencies or for something weird. We've never had any problems. No one who wasn't invited is going to get through the gate, and Dad isn't a worrier!" She laughed. "I think he's certain his reputation alone is enough to keep people in line. Besides, these people know better than to go through and start opening closed doors, but lots of the rooms are open. There's a lot of staff to help everyone around."

"Will there be dancing?" he said and gestured toward a dance floor by the orchestra.

"Oh, yes. Definitely. That's always a big part of the parties. People love to drink and have a good time, and Mom and Dad are good hosts. Will you dance with me later?"

"Of course I will," he said absently, holding her hand, still looking around the crowd, awed by the wealth and elegance. "Wait. Holy shit. I just had a thought. Will Christopher Walken be dancing? In front of me?"

She laughed. "I don't know. He might. Come on, let's get to the bar and get you a drink."

They were enjoying themselves, and everyone was on their best behavior. The two of them had a glass or two of champagne and some appetizers, offered by several of the passing waiters. Carey, who wore a form fitting, fully-sequined backless dress, eventually sauntered over to them and gave Charlotte a subtle up-down and said, "I see you are still playing the innocent little girl in that silly skirt, embracing your ingénue." She smirked at her sister, smiled coyly at David, and waited for her reaction.

"Yup! I like having fun and feeling light. Light of spirit, Carey. You should try it sometime. So where is your date?" Charlotte said as she looked around, trying to change the subject.

"Whatever," said Carey, rolling her eyes. "Harley's over there, but he's not my date, date, more like one of the crowd." She shrugged. "We're friends. He's so much older than I am, but god knows he's gorgeous to look at in the morning," she said as she took another swig of her drink.

"I'm a little surprised Mom and Dad are letting you drink," said Charlotte. "You're barely old enough."

"God, you're such a downer! What are you, like a Quaker person or something, Charlotte? Christ, I'm old enough to drink if I want to. The French let their kids drink at sixteen, and I'm eighteen. I can do whatever I want now. What do you care anyway, you're never around here."

Spinning her attention to David, Carey said, "Daaavid," as she turned in a circle and pouted at him over her shoulder. "How do you like my dress?"

Recognizing the danger, David said, "You look very beautiful, Carey. You both do."

"Um hmmm," she said, nodding her head as if she'd won some contest.

"Well, I'll see you around, kids," she said as she left them.

Charlotte gave her naked back a stony glare as David watched her wiggle away. "Okay!" said David, positioning himself in front of Charlotte, blocking the view. "Hey, that was fun. Don't mind her, though, okay? You're the most beautiful woman here this evening." David kissed her lips tenderly. Standing close he said, "I need to use the restroom, would you mind if I left you alone for a few?"

"No. Go ahead. I'm going to visit with Mom and Dad."

He kissed her again and departed.

Walk like you haven't a care in the world, David, he counseled himself. *Walk as if this were your home, and you had every right to wander.*

He had to scope out the walkway to Henry's office. He had to know if that part of the house was cordoned off or if security was positioned nearby. His heart pounded as he made his way back inside and in the right direction. Past the yellow sala with the Cantera stones housing the price-less Diego Rodríguez de Silva Velázquez, he walked down a breezeway unmolested and saw that the way to Henry's office was clear. He stood outside the closed door, staring at it, wondering if anyone could possibly be inside. He knew it was early yet and some time before they would depart, but he might not have another chance. He took it.

He walked up to the door and turned the handle. It wasn't locked. He peered into the darkened room and walked quickly inside, shutting the door quietly behind him. He stopped to turn on a light as he made his way over to the cabinet. Remembering the stupid code he hoped he correctly saw Mr. Carrows enter into the security panel, he plugged it in, and it magically opened. He then simply switched the real stone with the paste he had in his breast pocket. Why that man had trusted him and allowed him to view the security procedure was a mystery to David, but one for which he was truly grateful. He looked at the paste in the cabinet and was amazed at its likeness to the original. It would take a trained eye and loupe to see the difference, and when you weren't looking for a problem, you usually didn't see one. He hoped. He'd lied a bit to Henry when he said the paste didn't compare to the real one. Peter Carl Fabergé didn't earn his legendary status by making anything second rate. It looked perfect. Thank god Julia wasn't wearing it tonight.

His throat felt dry, his palms sweaty as he closed the door on the cabinet. The deed was done. He quickly turned off the light and exited the room, walking with a controlled gait back down the long stone corridor until he was just outside of the yellow sala. He heard voices and came to a dead stop.

The distinctive, gravelly whisper of Christopher Walken, his voice oddly halting in his own unique manner, was shocking and unmistakable.

"It could have been mine. Henry and I. We had them. I said to him. Where do we go? From heere. What do we do? With this conundrum?"

"Then what happened?" said an interested female voice.

"Then. I said to him. Henry. Let me ask you a question. My mother. Made cobbler. Did your mother? Did she make cobbler for you. Henry? And do you know. What he said?"

"What?" whispered the female voice.

"He said. He wasn't interested. In cobbler."

There was a long pause. David, confused, listened raptly.

"I see," said the female voice.

David had no idea what was going on, but he knew he needed to get back to Charlotte and out of the area. He shook himself out of his trance and headed down, walking by in a fast but measured pace. His heart hammering, he succeeded in safely passing the sala and made it, eventually, intact, back to the party. There was no turning back now.

The rest of the evening went by in a blur. He held his anxiety in check until it was time to leave. Their bags were already packed and in the back of a chauffeured car waiting to take them to the airport.

"I'm so glad you made the trip, honey," Julia said as she hugged Charlotte goodbye in the front door atrium.

"David, it was a pleasure meeting you," Henry said as he held a gold box in his hands and extended it toward him. "One of our parting gifts." He continued, "We give them to all the guests as a memento for attending."

"Thank you, sir," said David, taking the box. "It was great getting to meet all of you."

"Goodbye, David," said Julia, her hands at her throat, emotional, not reaching out. David bowed his head in her direction once more and said, "Thank you, Mrs. Carrows. Thank you for your kind hospitality."

They turned and left.

He'd done it. By god, he'd done it. He couldn't even believe it himself. He'd pulled it off. He had the Fancy, the *real* Fancy in his pocket. Just casually in his damn pocket. He couldn't believe that Alexandra Romanov's ring was in his possession. He felt huge! Alive! A part of history and the world.

And now he and Charlotte were back on a plane, still in their party clothes, flying through the black night toward home.

Distracted, each for their own very different reasons, they had yet to open the gold box they'd received as a parting gift from Henry. David pulled it out.

"We should open this," he said quietly.

"Go ahead," she said, as they huddled together in the small space.

David opened the gold-wrapped box. Inside was nestled another gold box but this one artistically engraved. He pulled it out.

"Oh, this is cool," he said as he opened it.

Surprised that it illuminated when opened, he saw that it contained a gold-plated replica of a one-hundred-dollar bill nestled in a satin bed. It was quite beautiful.

"Oh, wow," said David picking up the gold brick and feeling its weight. "Is this real? It looks real. They gave one of these to everyone who was at the party?" he said with amazement.

"It does look real, doesn't it?" she said as he passed it to her. She smiled at him. "So, what do you think it's worth, David?"

"I don't know, it could be pretty valuable. The box is almost more interesting than the gold bar. The way it glows when you open it? Really, really cool."

"Let me ask you a question. Say you didn't know me and were just a guest at the party and when you left, you got this gift. What would you do with it?"

"I don't know. I'd show it to my friends. Maybe check to see if it was real."

"Exactly." She laughed. "Daddy likes his little games. I suppose we might have the real one, but I guess we won't know until we check it out. Mom and Dad have always given gifts after their parties, and the fun part is that one of the guests will receive a very real, expensive piece, but the others will be replicas. I think Dad likes the thought of his guests running around LA to various jewelers, trying to determine if they got the real thing or not. I used to think it was insulting, like he was laughing at them, the marionette lord, still pulling the strings, manipulating people for the sport of it, but now, I'm not so sure. I think it's fun, especially since the word is out, and everyone is in on it."

"Really? Huh. That's interesting."

David looked back at the gold bar and thought about all the expense and trouble Henry went to, to play his little game. He laid the gold piece back in the box and closed it, putting the box back inside his backpack. He lay his head back on the seat, closed his eyes, and smiled. He enjoyed the irony that Mr. Carrows would play a game of chance with his guests while he was playing a very real shell game with him, too.

He thought back over the last few days. He'd had many opportunities to obtain the replica at the Met before leaving town but to be on the safe side, did so only the day before they left in case for some stupid reason someone looked for it. But he hadn't really believed that would happen.

At the Metropolitan Museum of Art, it was the responsibility of each department to make inventories in only one- to five-year cycles. Exceptions went through the director's office. And David knew that after the Romanov Jewels exhibit ended, the fake Fancy was put back into storage and placed on a list for deaccession. This meant the Met considered the item no longer an interest for research or study or auditing.

It was a constant weeding process for an evolving inventory in the monstrously huge museum. Amongst the thousands of obscure pieces, David had purposefully placed the ring in the wrong box, the right box empty, which could appear to be a clerical error if someone ever searched for it. David needed to make sure he had control over its location. He needed exclusive access to it. If someone looked for it, they would never find it without him. He'd waited until the morning they left before he went back and took it. Now it was gone forever.

The next part of his plan was in place as well. He'd prepared everything and had worked over the details with a thorough exhaustion. It was all coming together. He was proud of himself.

After they reached the townhome early Monday morning, David showered and changed his clothes for work. Grabbing only his backpack, he made his way back to their bed to say goodbye to Charlotte.

"Roll over here and give me a hug, you. I'm off to work. I'm glad to be home but really glad we took the trip. You're glad too, right?" he said, searching her eyes.

"I am. Thanks again for convincing me to go. You were right. It broke the ice, and that feels really good. You've been so good for me, David." She put her arms up, her hands on each side of his head, pulling him down to her.

"You're welcome," he said and kissed her. He stood, looking down on her smiling, sleepy face and said, "Bye, honey, I'll miss you." He left the room.

She would never see him in her home again.

Chapter 7

_____

That Monday evening after David didn't come home from work and wasn't returning her texts, Charlotte began to worry. As the evening wore on, she started to become concerned that something bad had happened to him. Tuesday morning when David still hadn't returned home, she was finally able to get someone on the phone at the Met. After speaking with them, she was surprised to learn that there had been no meeting the day before, and in fact, no one had seen David on Monday at all.

They were worried as well. She didn't know what to think until the mail arrived on Tuesday afternoon, and there was an envelope addressed to her written in a hand she recognized. It was from David. She ripped open the envelope and dropped to her knees in disbelief upon reading:

"Dear Charlotte, I'm sorry to tell you this in this manner, but I didn't have the courage to say these words to your face. I'm leaving you, the Met, and the country to be with my parents. I made the decision some time ago that my life

was and should be with them and not with you and a future that I was unsure of. I'm sorry I hurt you in this way, but I have to do what I think is best for me. Maybe someday you will understand. Goodbye. Please don't try to find me. Forgive me. David."

"You son of a bitch," she said and fainted.

———————————

Incredulity and horror that Charlotte was dumped by David overwhelmed her. Shock and disbelief that this was even happening rolled over her in waves the next few days as she dealt with his unbelievably harsh betrayal and abandonment. She felt sick all the time. And she had never felt so alone in all her life. Except she wasn't alone. The next blow came when she realized she was pregnant.

She didn't know how to handle that either. She was rocked by another devastating upheaval of emotions as she weighed her anger at David and the thought of having his baby. She didn't know if she could do it. But her inertia and physical illness kept her down and barely coping until one day she decided she'd had enough. Enough of David's actions destroying her soul. Enough of wallowing in her pain and enough indecision. She pushed through her anger at David and formed a clear vision that she needed to care for her body and the growing child. The thought of becoming a mother became a full-time distraction, which brought her through the worst of her grief over David's deceit and departure.

As the months crept along, she got stronger and prepared her home for the baby. She was going to be a mom. It was unbelievable.

One afternoon, well into her final trimester, she was in a baby store finalizing the purchase and delivery of the crib.

She'd enjoyed converting a bedroom into a nursery and decorating it. Not knowing if she was carrying a boy or a girl, a couple of her friends had thrown her a shower, giving her items in colors of pastel green and buttercup yellow. She loved buying all the tiny clothes and socks and shoes and had almost everything prepared, waiting for her and her baby at home. Her secret home.

It was exhausting making up stories when her friends, pity in their eyes, worried about her. She'd made up a family for their sakes and felt terrible for lying to them.

She listened to the conversation of two women nearby.

"Mom," the pregnant girl said, laughing. "We already have more clothes than she'll ever wear! She'll grow faster than she can put them on."

Charlotte gave them a quick glance and watched as the mom, her arms loaded with baby girl clothes leaned over her daughter's stomach and said, "You don't mind that your grandma is going to spoil you, do you?"

Charlotte felt a little sick and grabbed the counter. After finishing the transaction, she left the store, eager to be alone with her swelling emotions. Among a host of other feelings, she was overwhelmed by sadness and fear. Her mother and none of her family even knew she was pregnant.

She knew it wasn't natural, in fact, it felt shameful. But it had gotten away from her, and she didn't know what to do. She saw her reflection in the glass of a building on the street. She couldn't believe how far it had gone. She'd been so shocked and embarrassed that David had left her. How could she admit that he didn't even have the decency to do it to her face? That he'd sent a letter to her in the mail? She hadn't heard from him since.

She'd been afraid to tell her family that she'd been so completely wrong about him. She knew their reaction would be brutal, so she chose not to tell them. Then, when she found out she was pregnant, her world had spun so far off-balance that she lost her way.

As the months wore on, she'd had fleeting moments, her hand poised over the phone to call her mom, but she always hesitated. They'd spoken many times, but Charlotte didn't know how to open up. She didn't know how to begin to seek their help, to admit that she'd been so stupid about David. She also didn't want to talk about David in general. She'd worked hard to win back her strength, her equilibrium, and happiness, and his memory was like a festering sore she wanted to forget. But here she was, about to give birth, and her parents didn't know. She wasn't going to be able to keep it secret. Obviously. But she'd been dreading the call.

She put a hand on her stomach and wondered who was growing inside of her. Each day, her baby got a little stronger, a bit bigger, making their presence known as a real live human being. The doctor told her she'd been the perfect pregnant mom and that both she and the baby were healthy. She already loved her child. She also took comfort knowing that even though she'd be a single mother, they had resources, more than enough to survive.

But what about the delivery? Who would be there with her for that? She couldn't imagine going through it alone. It didn't make any sense. Her friends had offered their support, and she was grateful for that, but it wasn't the same as family. She'd been vague with everyone, uncertain about what to do.

She got back to the townhouse, locked the door, and lumbered up the stairs to the baby's room. Sitting in the glider and looking around at all the lovely pieces, the toys, the bottles, the odd paraphernalia that she was told would be important, she knew she was ready. Physically.

She began to cry. She rocked, holding her face in her hands, calling out, "Mom..." The person, the only person in the world, who she knew she desperately wanted to be there.

"Put it away, Charlotte!" she yelled at herself. "Forget everything. She's your mom. She'll forgive you for not telling her. She'll understand what happened. Dad might not, but she's got to understand. Just call her!"

When Charlotte finally did call her, it all came out, and her mom listened. She didn't judge her, at least not at that moment, and she got on a plane and came to her. Petunia Carrows McGee was born, and she was immediately loved by them both.

———————————

Petunia brought into Charlotte's world a love Charlotte had only dreamed about. Being a mother was an experience that expanded her and gave her hope and utter happiness. Charlotte was healthy and strong and finally able to look back at the first few months after David's exit as just a bad dream. She found her and Petunia's days so fulfilling and exhausting that she rarely spent time dwelling on David. She and her daughter had a new life now, and they would move forward and fully embrace it. She now believed that the only reason David was ever even placed in her life was to bring about the birth of her daughter. He became a ghost she only felt vague ambivalence toward.

The day to day life of being a new mom was more than enough for Charlotte, but she was proud of herself that she also managed to finish her education. With the help of a part-time nanny, she graduated from NYU, but once that was accomplished, she was unsure about what direction she should take with her future. But then, fate stepped in to give her some guidance.

When Petunia was a little over two years old, Charlotte's mother called her with some news. Apparently, an insurance agent and their experts were doing an audit of the artwork and valuables in the Carrows's home and came across the fact that the Tsarina's Fancy was not authentic, it was a fake.

"We were stunned! Your father was outraged and couldn't believe it was true, but they had him look at it with a jeweler's loupe, and even he could see they were right."

"What are you saying? That's incredible! How did that happen? Did Sotheby's sell him a fake at auction?" she said, sitting down in the glider, watching as Petunia played with some toys.

"Apparently not. That was the first thought that came into his head too, but the insurance agent assured him that the last time they did an assessment of the jewels, the ring was authentic. So, the ring in the case was originally the real stone, but at some time, at some point, someone switched it with a paste replica."

"That's unbelievable, Mom. How would they even have access to it? Was anything else stolen or swapped?"

"No, that was the only item in the house that was tampered with. Your father is furious."

"I'll bet," Charlotte said as she recalled his steely anger and disposition. And for him of all people to be robbed, tricked, it was unthinkable. He would be out for blood.

"Do you guys have thoughts about what happened?" she said, idly picking up a stuffed bear and looking at it.

"As a matter of fact, your father has given this a great deal of consideration and has narrowed it down to a couple of possibilities. He believes that either you and David or David alone, swapped the stone the last time you were out here."

"What? Are you kidding me? I would never do that! Why would I? And David, how could he have done that? He didn't know where it was kept or the combination to the safe. For all his evil, he wasn't a jewel thief for god's sake." She jumped up from the chair and walked out of the room, worried her tone would upset Petunia.

"Charlotte. We aren't just considering you and him. We are factually accusing you and him. The facts are that when you were here, your dad gave David a tour of the home including the cabinet with the Tsarina's Fancy. David made a point to ask your father about it because he had been in contact with the replica at the Met during the Romanov Jewels exhibition. Stop and think about that now. He had access to the fake one, and he apparently had access to the cabinet because he swapped the ring, and as you are painfully aware, he then disappeared from your life the next day."

Charlotte felt as if someone had punched her. She leaned a hand on the wall for support. All the blood drained from her face and like a bout of vertigo, she was swimmingly brought back to the party and David's hasty departure. *My god, oh my god. This can't be happening. If he did this, if he did this then he was planning it for weeks. He not only intended to leave me, but he planned to rob us first.* She felt physically ill. "He betrayed me, Mom! And now I'm finding out he didn't just betray me by leaving, he robbed us as well?" She tried to lower her voice, but it was difficult.

"Your father thinks you might have helped him."

"What?" Charlotte pulled back from the phone, stunned, finally processing the full import of her mother's words. "Why would I do that? What are you talking about?"

"We all know how strained things were between us before you suddenly decided to visit. Maybe you wanted to hurt us or wanted to play a big joke on us or get revenge for all the things you hate us for? Maybe David convinced you to do it for the money, and you went along with him because you're unhappy with your allowance?"

"Mom, he left me! He fucking left me the next day! Remember? I didn't have anything to do with this!" She looked quickly into the nursery, and seeing that Petunia was all right, she ran down the hall to get some distance as her mom continued to admonish her.

"If you didn't, then you were brutally conned. And your father is furious with you that in his words, 'You were so lost in your mindless dreamy world that you didn't even bother to open your eyes and see the truth about your deadbeat boyfriend.'"

Charlotte was crying. This was too much. God, just another reminder that her relationship with her family was so stupid and broken that they would *accuse her* and hurt her when she was devastated enough by this second assault of treachery from David.

"Mom, I swear to you I had nothing to do with it. David tricked me. He deceived me. I get it. I get that I was stupid. But I loved him, and I thought he loved me. He told me he loved me! We dated for two years! I thought I knew him, but I obviously didn't. I'm sorry this happened, but please, don't hurt me too. I don't know how to make this better, but please don't accuse me like this. You were here for Petunia's birth, Mom! Remember that time we spent together? I was so happy you were here, that we shared that. I really did think we could all try to be better to each other. I wanted that. I wasn't secretly laughing into the back of my hand that I'd conned you and Dad and stole from you at the party. God, I just wouldn't do that! You know me! Right?" she said, incredulous.

"I really don't know what to think. Your dad is out for blood right now. I can't calm him down. He told me to tell you that he is cutting you off. Financially and otherwise. He is cutting off your allowance and your credit cards. He also said he didn't want to report the theft because he didn't want the family scandal out there for the world to see. He has his pride and his reputation to consider. But he said he can't forgive you."

She was just reeling. Again. Another blow. Her tenuous family relations, gone. David, screwing her over, again. And now money. Gone.

"Mom, I can't believe you're saying this. Mom, really? What are you thinking? Do you think that's fair? That I deserve that? I didn't have anything to do with this," she croaked. "I was devastated by David, you know that! Think about everything he did to me. Are you going to hurt me too? Do I really deserve that?" She was shaking, a tremble inside her; her teeth actually began to chatter.

"I don't know what to think. I really don't. I know your father is right, at least on some level. We have been patient with you for years. He feels if you so desperately want to not be a part of this family, then it is time you started making it on your own. He has never even met Petunia!"

"Mom! You and Dad can come to New York to visit any time you want!"

"It's all a part of *you* making the effort, Charlotte. He doesn't want to have to come to you. He wants you to come to us. And your sister hasn't met Petunia either."

"You know that's separate. You know we don't get along," she said as the tears ran down her face.

"Maybe if you tried harder. Put in some effort, that would change as well. Your dad is just really, *really* angry. He said he is fed up. I can't control him, and I'm not going to get in the way. At least not right now. He is just too upset."

"Okay, Mom. Thanks for trying!"

"I'll let you go. Good luck. I'm sure you'll be fine. I'll be in touch. I will. I'm just so torn and confused right now, Charlotte. I'll be in touch. Goodbye."

And just like that, Charlotte's world changed again. And her hatred for David that she had worked so hard to bury returned, with a vengeance.

Chapter 8

When David Torres left Charlotte, he flew directly to Dubai. He'd saved enough money for the trip, thanks to his low overhead while living with Charlotte and his job at the Met. He could afford to get to Dubai and stay in one of the cheaper hotels for about $150 a night. His passport was up to date thanks to his parents' recent move to Mexico, and he had few personal belongings that couldn't be replaced. Most importantly, he'd made sure Victor Al Nahyan was available and interested in meeting with him.

Off the plane in Dubai, he contacted Victor and set up a meeting. They met at a hotel bar on the mall not far from the gigantic Burj Al Arab Jumeirah. The iconic sail-shaped hotel built on an artificial island was connected to the mainland by a private bridge. Its huge presence trumpeted a message of Arabian wealth on the Persian Gulf.

David sat across from the large, burly man, who seemed pleased to see him. David was nervous, his foot shaking under the table, but eventually, he got to the purpose of the visit and asked Victor if he was still interested in the stone.

"The Tsarina's Fancy we spoke about? The one from the exhibition? Yes, it has always intrigued me. Why do you ask?"

"I happen to know that you could acquire the real one. It's for sale," David said carefully.

"Really? I don't understand, is the Met reacquiring it? Is it going to auction? I hadn't heard that," he said, confused.

"No. It's not going to auction. It is available right now, for private purchase," he said with intent.

"I don't understand this. Is Henry Carrows putting it up for sale? Why are you here? Are you representing them? I didn't know the Met had a relationship with that despicable man."

"No. The Met is not involved with this. And no, I am not representing the Carrows family. I am saying that the stone, the Fancy, the real Tsarina's Fancy, is available for purchase, today, through me." He looked at Victor to gauge his reaction. Everything hinged on this moment.

David watched the gears turn in Victor's head. He could see his confusion.

His look askance, Victor replied with suspicion, "I'm not sure what is going on here my *friend*, David Torres. I'm not sure what to think about what you are saying to me."

"I'm going to tell you something, my good friend, Victor Al Nahyan. As you know, I had access to the paste replica of the ring at the Met, and it turned out, I also had access to the real one. And when the opportunity came, I took it, and I switched the stones. Mr. Henry Carrows is now unknowingly in possession of the fake, a copy of the Tsarina's Fancy."

Victor looked stunned. He stared wide-eyed at David and said, "I find this difficult to believe. How would you trick a man like Henry Carrows? How do you know him? How would you have access to the ring for that matter?"

"Fate. Fate, mostly, and the details are not relevant. But I remembered that you had an interest and preoccupation with the stone. You had a deep personal passion for the ring, and you had regret that you didn't purchase it at auction when you had the chance. Secondly, I remembered that you had a mild obsession with Mr. Henry Carrows. For your own reasons, you told me that you hated the man. I am here today to help you correct both of those circumstances. You may purchase the ring from me and at the same time screw over Mr. Henry Carrows. Today." David took his index finger and tapped it on the table, then waved it through the air and relaxed into his chair, crossing his legs with confidence.

Mr. Al Nahyan sat back in his chair, momentarily silent. Twisting a ring slowly around his finger, he looked at David with hooded, menacing eyes.

"So, you have committed a crime in the United States and robbed Mr. Henry Carrows. Is this all correct?" he said darkly.

"Yes, it is," said David, nodding.

"And you are saying you have the Tsarina's Fancy on you, right now, as we speak." He flippantly gestured. "And you wish to sell it to me?"

"That is partially correct. I wish to sell the stone to you, Victor, but the Fancy is not with me at this moment."

"What makes you think I won't just take the ring from you when it's in my possession, my friend, the thief?" Victor leaned in. "You come into Dubai, alone." He gestured around. "And believe you are in charge? I am a man of influence here, and you are not."

David had been worried about this too, but he played the last card in his hand. "Because I think you are a man of integrity and tradition. Because you believe Henry Carrows is not. I've met him. I know him, and you were right about that. He is despicable. He deserves to be shamed and robbed. If you buy the ring, then you will have the pleasure of shaming him, and I think that alone is something you would pay for. I suppose you could overpower me and rob me too." David shrugged. "But that means you are no better than he."

Victor was silent a moment. "I see. And what did you have in mind as a price for this stolen piece of jewelry and my personal satisfaction in bringing Henry Carrows pain?"

Victor was almost there. David could feel it. He just had to make this last step, and he would be free.

"I thought I would set the price for exactly half of what Mr. Carrows purchased it for. $1,750,000. Cash."

Victor didn't blink.

"$1,750,000 cash. Payable to you for the Fancy." He sat back and considered. But not for long.

"I think you are very lucky that you came to me, David. You are a thief, but I am a fair man. I will not rob you. My soul will remain clean. Unlike yours, but that is now your problem and not mine. If someday you lose your hand for this, that is the price you alone will pay. Yes, David, I will agree to this price. I will be very happy to be the owner of this treasured item. I will not make the same mistake twice. And it will bring me great happiness to know that Mr. Henry Carrows has been deceived. When he discovers he has been robbed, he will be unhappy and look for revenge. Will you be prepared for that?"

"Let me worry about that," he said coolly.

"If and when he discovers that the Fancy is in my possession, he will surely ask my associates some questions," he said with some concern.

"You can simply say that you were made aware that it was for sale from a friend who assured you it was on the market quietly. These things happen from time to time. You had no reason to believe that there was anything wrong with the purchase. And, if Mr. Carrows wanted to pursue this he would have to go through the courts, which for various reasons I assure you he will not want to do. As you are most likely aware, he is very prideful and will be too embarrassed to air this situation in public. He has a reputation to uphold, and his massive ego would not let him."

Victor Al Nahyan smiled. Delighted. "You are right, my good friend, the thief, David Torres. You are right."

And with that, the details were arranged. Mr. Al Nahyan verified that the jewel was real, and the money was wired to a bank in Rio de Janeiro per David's instructions. After David verified the money was in the bank, he gave the ring to the happily gregarious Victor. David had one other item he negotiated before the exchange, he needed a new identity. This was not a problem for Victor Al Nahyan.

Chapter 9

Charlotte was not going to break. Not again. Never again. And not over stupid David, who was beyond contempt. She worked hard to stop herself from the mental torture of trying to determine when exactly David's plan was put into place. At what point had he stopped loving her? At what point did he decide to grab the replica ring from the Met and swap it with the real one at Whispering Cliffs? He couldn't have thought of it suddenly. He must have been planning for some time, just waiting for his opportunity. The pieces, in painful retrospect, fell into place, but it only gave her heartache to remember.

She was more upset by her parents blaming her and accusing her of somehow helping David rob them. It was unbelievable that they would think this. She knew things were strained with them and that she should have made more of an effort to include them in her and Petunia's life, but something always held her back.

The first couple of years away from them all was a new experience, and during that time she began to find her identity as a young woman. The pressure of being brought up as a rich girl in California wasn't too bad when she lived among them in her privileged community, but she'd been aware from an early age that people treated you differently if you were very wealthy. They were more careful and conciliatory. They wanted to please you and compliment you on the smallest thing. Charlotte had also seen her rich friends treat those less advantaged than them badly. Staff and teachers and people who worked for a living were often taken for granted and looked down upon.

Charlotte observed this behavior from her friends and family and knew she did not want to be a part of that mindset and social clique. She believed in order to find herself she needed to find out how the world really worked and how it was experienced by others than the extremely privileged. And she needed to get away from her friends and especially her family to accomplish this. She felt it was important to keep the fact that she was a Carrows a secret so it wouldn't influence others' perceptions or interactions with her. She also knew if people saw her townhome, they would automatically know that she was rich, and she didn't want that influence affecting her relationships and achievements. It was one of the reasons she always referred to her townhome as an apartment.

It became relatively easy to get into the habit of not going home to California and distancing herself from the family. Her siblings had very little interest in her now that she was out of their shooting range, and her dad was always busy with one project or another. He was also quick to jump into any conversation with some inflammatory and prejudicial comment about some event or person or group, and this too always kept the tension high and the atmosphere challenging. Her mom, in Charlotte's opinion, was too passive and always had been about her family. Charlotte felt that her mother should have stepped in any number of times over the years to help ease tensions or set the record straight or punish someone or intervene. And Charlotte was a little angry with her for this.

After David left, her world had fallen apart. She was extremely disturbed by the fact that she had been so completely wrong about someone. It wasn't like her, but she had let her guard down after she left home and walked the path of anonymous Charlotte McGee. She mistakenly assumed her anonymity would protect her. But that was what she wanted. That was the point of being anonymous; she could be trusting because no one knew who she really was. And yet she'd still chosen badly. Maybe she should have listened to her dad more often. Maybe he was onto something.

But then Petunia was born, and her heart was healed. In fact, her heart had never felt so big in her life. She was now filled with another and different kind of love. And it was enough. She loved her daughter with all of her being. She spent her days getting to know this little person who had been given to her. The sleepless nights and the worry about how to cut her nails and bathe her properly and the right type of sunblock and her nutrition and the myriad of things that Charlotte had never thought about consumed their days.

The stroller she purchased was put to good use as they traveled the city and saw the sights. Charlotte pointed out every blade of grass and dog and flower, and the sun and stars to this new creature. They would travel to the park and restaurants and eventually, Charlotte knew that sooner than she realized, she would need to start thinking about classes and schools. She didn't have any idea where to enroll Pinky in the city, so she realized she needed to open herself up to other moms to find out how it all worked.

She joined a gym that had a nursery, and the two of them went there to learn. Pinky had a chance to see and play with other children while Charlotte had a chance to visit with other moms and learn from them all the tips and strategies that keep a mother's world's wheels greased. She also set up playdates for Pinky and opened herself up to new friend-ships. She knew she needed to do this, not only for herself but for her daughter. It was one thing for Charlotte to be a moderate recluse, but she would not presume this nor foist this onto her lovely daughter who deserved to be shown the world.

During those first two years, they went to the zoo and Gymboree classes. She took Pinky swimming and got her acclimated to the water so she would be comfortable with it and learn the life skill of swimming. They had been happy, and Charlotte was contented, at least temporarily, to play stay-at-home mom. When she wasn't with her daughter, she was in school finishing her degree at NYU. They were busy years. She had her home and allowance, and they would be fine.

But her parents had given her life another painful twist. They not only hurt her heart, but they'd forced her into another reality. The only reality she had ever known was one in which money had never been an object. The idea that she might need to financially support herself was a wild scenario she'd oddly never considered. That the money and privileges she had always taken for granted would be purposefully taken away from her was frightening. She didn't expect her family would ever do this to her because she believed, that even with the difficulties between them, they were still a family. To cut off her allowance as a punishment for something she did not do was not right. It angered Charlotte that her parents would be so shortsighted and hurtful. The news that David had robbed them was not just horrendous to them, it was to her as well. She was horrified that David, someone she thought she knew so well, was capable of another even deeper level of despicable behavior. David's thievery was another blow to Charlotte, and her parents should see it would be punishment enough. This was Petunia's father, and his depraved behavior would always be in her mind. David would be there forever, whether she liked it or not.

She had to make some decisions. If she was going to be cut off, she would need money to survive, which meant she would need to go out and make it. Whatever it took. She'd get a job, a good job, and forge a life for herself and Pinky alone. And to hell with her wretched family and vile David. She would never see them again.

Chapter 10

Charlotte's mother, Julia Carrows, had always been a beautiful woman. In her youth, she was a dancer in a traveling ballet company from the Ukraine. When Henry Carrows met the lovely, talented, lithe, and worldly young girl in Los Angeles, he fell in love with her on their first meeting. Julia was an accepting person, resigned and slightly self-involved, but she was also resilient, which was a necessary trait to survive the turmoil that came with being a family member in the Carrows household. While she typically made choices based on taking the least aggravating path, she had grown weary of the constant fighting and separateness in her family. Her children were basically a mess. Charles and Carey were drama makers who kept her off-balance well into their adulthoods, which should have brought with it maturity and wisdom. She was often confused when reflecting on her children and had regret that she had let it all go so far off path.

Charlotte, of all the children, resembled Julia the most. Julia had always had a soft spot in her heart for Charlotte, but she was more of a realist than her daughter. After her marriage, Julia's life was built around her husband, and she had been content to have it that way. It was a perfect match for Henry as well since he always wanted to be in control.

But where was Charlotte? Charlotte McGee for god's sake. So different from the other two that she actually changed her name. They all supported her decision to attend college, and NYU was a wonderful school, but of course, it was across the country. And once Charlotte left for school, the siren call of home was too distant to reach her. And Julia was convinced she no longer even wanted to be reached.

Now, Julia sat alone in her favorite room at Whispering Cliffs, the upstairs sala. The Spanish tiles anchored by an antique Spanish rug in red hues and the massive Douglas fir beams on the ceiling gave the room a warmth and comfort that she craved. Wrapped in a blanket, she gazed into the fire crackling in the stone and plaster hearth and wondered how it could have all gone so wrong. She was miserable as she began to accept the fact that her family was broken. She was crying when Henry came into the room.

She turned her face to avoid looking at him.

He said, "Julia? I haven't seen you all day. What are you doing up here?"

"Nothing. I'm doing nothing, Henry. I'm just sitting here wondering how our lives could go so wrong. Look at us," she said, gesturing around the room and out the window toward the ocean. "We have everything! People, everyone we know, probably think we have it all. We're the luckiest people on the planet. But you know what? They'd be wrong. Do you think we have it all, Henry? Is there anything missing from our lives? This beautiful life that so many people envy?"

Henry stepped into the room and gazed around. He took some time to collect his thoughts and walked to the window, looking out at the sea. He turned to her, finally, sighing. "What's missing, Julia?"

She looked into his face, incredulous that he wouldn't know the answer to her question.

"You know what I'm talking about, Henry. Don't speak to me as if you don't understand how I feel. My entire life I have been pushing myself to create success. First as a dancer, ripped apart from my family to become an athlete, next as your wife, pushing myself to make a great success of our marriage, always letting you take the lead, make our decisions so you could feel in control. Look at us! Rich beyond imagination, successful beyond imagination, intimidating to the world! You've built that, and I've helped you every step of the way. But what do we have, Henry? What do we really have? What has all the work, the hard work of pushing, always pushing, brought us? Are you happy, Henry?" She sat up, throwing the blanket aside. "Are you?"

Henry sat down across from her. "Julia, why are we having this conversation again? Why are you making yourself miserable? Yes, I am happy. We're happy, aren't we? You still love me, don't you?"

She shook her head as fresh tears ran down her face. "Henry," she whispered, "our family, our children, where are they?"

He sat back, clasped his hands together with patience and placed them between his knees. "Our children are fine. Charles lives with us most of the time. Doesn't he make you happy? Carey comes and goes, but she's with us too. You know that."

"Charlotte, Henry. Charlotte. And Petunia. You know who I'm talking about. They are not here. She is your daughter. Your granddaughter. Your only grandchild, and you've never even met her! Don't you want to see them? Don't you miss them?"

He stood up, his back to her at the fireplace. He waved an arm angrily in her direction. "I don't want to argue with you, Julia. We've had this discussion. Many times! Charlotte made her decisions. She chose to disassociate with her family. She made that decision all on her own. Her privacy, her unwillingness to visit us, she made that choice."

"We could have gone to her. We could have forced her to see that we cared about her, that we loved her. I know you never bought into the pain she said we inflicted on her, but the fact that she believed it, that she felt it, we should have tried to meet her halfway. We should have gone to her and even tried family counseling if that's what she needed to understand that we loved her."

"Family counseling!" He turned, clearly angry now. "Are you kidding me? We didn't need counseling. Maybe she did, but I'm not going to admit that we all did. Julia, you've got to get a handle on this. Charlotte chose to leave us. Now, maybe it won't be forever, I don't know, but has she reached out? Has she tried to contact you? No. That's your answer. She needs to grow up, so give her the time to do that, and when she's ready to apologize to us, we'll be here. She knows where to find us. Charles was out there just a few months ago and said she was fine. Really, if something horrible were to happen, I'd bet my last dollar that she'd call, but until then, the ball's in her court. She needs to come to us."

"To bend her knee to you?"

"Julia, that's not fair. That's not like you. Please don't take this out on me. I'm not the one who stole millions of dollars. I'm not the one who ignored us, even when she was pregnant. She didn't even call to tell us until it was almost time to deliver! Who does that?"

"She does that. She did that. She told me she was embarrassed, and I believed her. She told me she was devastated that David left her, and I believed her. And after Petunia was born, she was busy being a single mother and finishing her college education. She would have come to us then, I know she would have if we hadn't cut her off and blamed her for the robbery. I don't believe she had anything to do with it."

"You don't know that. But let's just say that it's true. She didn't know that creep was going to rob us. She brought him to us. She brought him into our home. She's out there in New York, thinking she's got it all figured out, but then she meets David, and boy can she pick 'em. After everything we tried to teach her about life, she chooses chose that guy. You would think that after he dumped her, she would realize that she needed her family more than ever. That we were right about everything. But does she? No. She still thinks she knows more about life than we do and stays away. She's hurt me too, Julia. You know that!"

"Then why didn't we do something about it? Why are we waiting for her to make the first move? Why can't you go to her, Henry? Break this impasse?" she begged.

"I won't. Our daughter, Charlotte *McGee*, needs to come to me."

Julia sat there, staring at her husband whose guidance she had followed so proudly, so confidently throughout their marriage and murmured in a strangled voice, "Oh, Henry, what if that never happens?"

He shook his head in defiance. "I always get my way, Julia. It will happen. When she's ready."

Julia was no longer convinced that Henry was right. It came to her that if she didn't step in and do something, things would be irrevocably strained and possibly severed forever. It had been almost eighteen months since they'd discovered the robbery. And since that time, after they cut Charlotte off, Julia had had time to think about what this meant. She should have guessed that Charlotte would use this punishment to harden herself against the family and resolve to be officially and forever done with them. If Charlotte had only come home with the baby to California, Henry would have changed his mind. She was certain they could have reconciled. But that didn't happen. And now Julia believed it would never happen.

Julia realized that she should have also been more compassionate about the hurt that her child felt when she learned what David had done. Initially, Julia had been on Henry's side in believing that enough was enough with her oldest daughter and that they needed to take a firm hand and give her an ultimatum. If Charlotte didn't want to be a part of the family, then so be it.

But it wasn't what Julia wanted. She regretted their behavior and realized that cutting her off hadn't been the way to bring Charlotte and her beloved granddaughter back into their lives. Henry was a hard man who was used to being in command over all the aspects of their lives. But in this case, he had been wrong. And she had been wrong as well. They had a right to be angry with Charlotte for creating a chasm of emotional and physical distance from them, and they had a right to murder David, but they shouldn't have kicked her while she was down. They should not have punished Charlotte after learning about David's deep level of betrayal.

So now, it was time to act. They'd had eighteen months of silence from their daughter, and it was too much. The painful stalemate had to end, and Julia began to formulate a plan.

Some days later, she was seated among a beautiful array of tastefully opulent flower arrangements in a romantic restaurant in Beverly Hills. She had a lunch appointment with Alexander Macchi. If she believed her friends, he was a trustworthy private detective who worked indirectly for the Carrows's LA law firm. Julia had found it distasteful that some of her friends used private investigators to look into the affairs of their spouses, but now she was in the market for someone to help her.

She arrived early and ordered a glass of rosé, eager for Mr. Macchi's arrival. When she saw a man making inquiries with the maître d', she concluded that it was probably him. She hadn't known what to expect. Alexander Macchi was tall and handsomely masculine. Wearing an impeccable suit with no tie, he looked like the TV actor from *ER*, Goran Visnjic. She'd actually met the actor once in person, and both of them had a graceful, understated polish that appealed to her.

"Mrs. Carrows," he said as he was shown to her table. He held out his hand and gave her a firm, gentle handshake. "Good afternoon, I'm Alex Macchi."

She looked up at him and smiled, chastising herself slightly about being carried away with the man's good looks. "Mr. Macchi. Very nice to meet you."

After he ordered a glass of pinot noir from the server, he turned back to Julia and said, "In our telephone conversation, you mentioned that you were looking for someone to help you find a thief. I thought that was an intriguing entreaty. I hope you took some time to check my references."

"Oliver Baach and my family go way back. He vouched for you. That's all I need," she said referring to the senior partner at their law firm of Baach, McKenzie & Blake.

"He's a good man. I'm glad that's settled. Why don't you begin then, Mrs. Carrows? Tell me about the job and what you hope to accomplish."

Julia had no practice sharing family secrets, but there was something about Alex's eyes that made her want to trust him. She took a leap and began the story when Charlotte left for college. As they ate lunch, she brought him through the years of scattered, stilted communication, the hope she felt when Charlotte came home with her boyfriend and how that hope had been shattered months later when Charlotte finally told them she was expecting to deliver a child.

"We were horrified that she had been pregnant, and she hadn't even told us. She told me that she was humiliated because David had left her the day they returned to New York after visiting with us. She said she'd been devastated and embarrassed, and was afraid that we would make her feel ashamed."

Julia, mildly horrified to be repeating the story, persevered. "Whether or not that would have actually happened, I cannot say. But Charlotte eventually asked for my help, and of course, I went to her. I was the only family member present when my granddaughter, Petunia, was born. She named her Petunia Carrows McGee. I guess we should have been grateful that she put our family name in there at all, but that's done now.

"But I left there encouraged. I thought that maybe the birth of our granddaughter would help bring her home, but she told us she was busy raising Petunia and she was finishing her college education at NYU. That all being true, she obviously could have found the time to come home if she'd wanted to. The thing is, I think she was still afraid of Henry, still worried about the shame of being a single mother, and she wanted Henry to come to her. Of course, he wanted *her* to come to *him.* It's all ridiculous. The next blow came when Petunia was a little over two. We had an insurance audit, and they discovered that one of our jewels was not real."

She took a large sip of her wine and finished explaining the rest of the sordid tale. "Which brings us to today. My family is no longer speaking with one another. It's official, and it will never change unless something is done. I miss my daughter. My granddaughter. My husband is a stubborn man, but he is the love of my life. I've been so torn, but I'm resolved now to do something about this mess. I think if we could find David and bring him to Henry, then he might get the poison out of his blood about being robbed. If Henry could confront him and exact his revenge on this waste of a human being in whatever way he found most appropriate, then he might forgive Charlotte, and they could return to at least being civil toward one another. And who knows? If that happened, and Charlotte and Petunia agreed to come home, there might be a chance for all of us to get past this." She felt very vulnerable, her emotions laid bare before the virtual stranger.

Alex reached over and took Julia's hand in a most natural way, certainly not gratuitous or insincere.

"I am sorry for the theft," he said. "But I can see your real concern is for your family."

Julia's lip quivered slightly, trying to hold her emotions in check.

Alex released her hand and said, "Mrs. Carrows. I'm sure it's been difficult for you to tell me so much about your family history. I don't take that lightly. I come from a large family myself and understand that there are always challenges. But what you're experiencing must be very difficult. I'm sure my mother would be in a great deal of pain if she couldn't see her daughter and grandchild. So, I respect your desire to fix this. I truly do. I'd like to help you and your family, but there are a few things that we need to discuss," he said in a kind yet professional manner.

Julia looked down and smoothed the napkin in her lap, knowing where this was going. "You mean about David being Petunia's biological father."

Alex nodded. "Finding David may be doable, and I'm happy to help you with that, but if we do, Charlotte is going to need to be involved. This is her daughter's father. He may or may not know that he has a child, and I'm sure Charlotte will have strong feelings about him either way. She really needs to be involved in this investigation. If you want to have an honest, open relationship with her, if you want closure and healing, then I really think she needs to be a part of this discussion."

"I don't know how to approach her," Julia said in desperation. "It's been so long. I don't even know how she's doing. Charles said she has a job and is doing fine, but I don't even know what that means. I don't really know what her life is like right now. I don't know how she is coping. If she is seeing anyone, what Petunia is doing! How is my granddaughter? I don't really know how Charlotte would feel about my plan to find David. But I've got to do something. Maybe I haven't thought this through." Julia stopped, frustrated that she was tearing up again in public. She finished quietly. "It's just unbearable to be this estranged."

Alex, softly confident, said, "How about we take this investigation in steps. At some point, I will need to meet Charlotte, but in the meantime, I'll see what I can find out about her life. I'll also launch a search for David Torres. It may take some time to find him, but I have confidence that I can. We won't need to tell Charlotte about the investigation until I locate David. Then we can put a plan together about next steps."

Julia brightened, encouraged that she had an ally, someone who would help her. "Thank you, Alex."

He continued, "We'll find David. We'll get him in front of Mr. Carrows, and we'll find a way to mediate the estrangement. I promise. If she's anything like you, I'm sure she's feeling the pain of her isolation from her family as well. I can't imagine it would be otherwise."

Julia nodded, picked up her napkin again, and dabbed at her eyes.

"All right then. I have enough to get started, and I'll be in regular contact with you. You're my client, and I'll keep you informed every step of the way. But, may I ask another question?" He didn't wait for her to respond. "When I find David Torres, what are you going to do with him?"

Julia blinked. "I honestly don't know, but I'm sure Henry will have some ideas."

Chapter 11

Alexander Macchi was originally from Brooklyn, New York. He was intrigued by this case and didn't think it would take too much effort to track down someone that he believed was an amateur thief. After his first cursory inquiries, he found a picture of David from his passport and confirmed with Julia that he was looking at the right person. From there, he had the resources to obtain David's social security number, which enabled him to do a full background check.

He found no criminal background, which supported his theory that David was an amateur, albeit a lucky one. He found the history of his home life and education, his parents' deportation, his employment history, his spending habits, some credit and banking history, and his social media presence, which oddly was the least revealing piece about him.

He did some research on the Tsarina's Fancy and the traveling exhibition of Romanov Jewels. He didn't think the exhibition itself would lend much to his search, but as it happened, it was currently in San Francisco. He would run up the coast to see it before he left for New York.

He wanted to interview the Metropolitan Museum of Art and speak with David's past employer and coworkers about him, but he was unsure whether they were even aware that the Tsarina's Fancy paste copy was missing. He was not sure he wanted to alert them to this. At least not yet. The Carrows, above all, wanted to keep this personal scandal quiet. Alerting the Met in any way might make the story, with its connection to the Carrows family and a Romanov jewel, a media attraction.

But there were other ways to find David. Alex knew David had stolen the jewel, and he assumed he had left the country the day he walked out on Charlotte. David had to have some plan about what to do with the stone. He had to have some stratagem about where to go and where he wanted to live. He must have assumed the theft would eventually be discovered by the Carrows. Did David fear they would contact the police and report the crime, which would make David worry about extradition, assuming he was living outside the US? Or did David believe the Carrows would not report the theft to protect their reputation and avoid a scandal?

It was one or the other, and Alex was betting that David understood that the Carrows would seek anonymity. They kept a fairly low profile for people in their position. So, if David was unconcerned about extradition, that would mean he could be anywhere in the world. Even living in the United States.

His parents were in Mexico, currently serving their ten-year time bar penalty most likely with the hope of one day returning to the United States. At least that is what was in their deportation sentencing file. Would David be in Mexico with his parents? Julia shared with Alex the contents of his goodbye letter, claiming that was his course. But that had to be a load of crap. David was a thief and had just stolen a famous diamond. He wouldn't get anywhere near his parents. He would be too easily found.

Alex knew several facts about David. That he stole the stone, that he surely sold the stone, that he seemed to have a passion for art, and that he had screwed over Charlotte and the Carrows. The stone was the key. He would start by following that.

The Tsarina's Fancy had been up for auction many years ago at Sotheby's. Alex was familiar with the famous auction house, and more importantly, had a connection at the house who would help him.

He met with his source and uncovered some interesting history about the activities on the day the auction took place, specifically about the bidders. Quite often, wealthy customers wished to remain anonymous, but in the case of the Tsarina's Fancy, it was made public that it was purchased by Henry Carrows. Apparently, Henry had no reason to keep his identity hidden for that transaction. In fact, it was just another PR point of interest that lent to the Carrows myth.

The auction that day was for the sale of family items owned previously by a Grand Duchess from Russia. She had passed away and left many of her valuables to relatives who apparently needed the money more than keeping the history in the family. The event was well advertised in certain circles, and the interest and bidding that day was active and highly profitable for both the auction house and the family. And if the confidential records from Sotheby's were correct, the Tsarina's Fancy had bidders from both the private sector and museum representatives; but as everyone knew, Mr. Henry Carrows won that day, bidding a startling $3,500,000 for the jewel. It was the other private sector bidders that interested Alex. And he had a list. It wasn't terribly long.

———————————

David Torres, or as he was now known, David Cordoza, lived in São Paulo, Brazil. He liked the idea that the city was considered the New York City of the Latin world. It was a vibrant place filled with cultural and rich architectural traditions and also considered the financial center of Brazil.

Portuguese was the official language spoken in Brazil, which created no problem for David to assimilate since he was fluent in Spanish. He was also drawn to the region's South American culture because he supposed it would have similarities to his Mexican heritage. The weather in São Paulo was rather tropical, but mild. Rio de Janeiro was only 270 miles away, and the beaches were some of the best in the world.

David Cordoza did worry, however, about money. He knew the $1,750,000 he got for the Tsarina's Fancy would not last forever if he spent it like a fool. He knew he needed to integrate himself into the city slowly, to find his way and find his next step before he invested in a home or settled somewhere. He also needed to keep a low profile while he kept a careful eye on the LA and NYC newspapers.

David found the traffic and congestion brutal as he began to explore his new home, but he found the cost of living wonderfully low in comparison to New York City. He moved around from hotel to hotel, which he had calculated he could easily afford to do for years if he chose to. For although he had wildly enjoyed his time in Charlotte's townhome and the refinement and luxury of living in an elegant home in a large city, David was used to small environments. For his entire life, except for the year he lived with Charlotte, he had lived only in his parents' dismal ranch house or his dorm room at NYU. He found he could acclimate himself just fine living on a small budget while he took the time he needed to find his footing on his path to greatness.

He enjoyed himself very much. He was happy. São Paulo had nearly a million students enrolled in its universities. São Paulo is both the name of the state, as well as a city, and the people born in the city of São Paulo are known as Paulistanos. Those born in the state of São Paulo, though not in its capital, are called Paulistas. David wanted to become a Paulistano, one of about eleven million people. The city had about 12,500 restaurants and, of course, world-class museums, art, and nightlife.

With money in the bank and no concerns for his day to day existence, David found the life of a full-time tourist to be to his liking. But he knew he needed to set up shop, as it were, and find a section of the city where he wanted to live and a job or vocation where he could continue to climb the ladder of success.

São Paulo was similar to most large cities, boasting many private museums as well as museums partially funded by the government. Private museums stayed alive by the generous contributions of corporations, individuals, and foundations. Those monies then paid for the upkeep, maintenance, personnel, security, restoration, renovation, and acquisitions, which were a museum's daily life. Once

David got his sea legs in the city and had visited nearly all of the important museums, he decided he might be able to be a benefactor and solicitor representative for a museum. He would build a reputation in the art world, rub shoulders with the artists and owners, and more importantly, the wealthy benefactors who would come to know him as *the Paulistano* to go to in the art community of this great city.

And if he had learned anything from Charlotte, it was that he needed the clothes. He spent a small fortune to obtain the right assemblage of expression for himself. He looked like a handsome man with fortune, education, and breeding. He attended openings, events, and eventually, parties. Invitations became abundant for a handsome, young, and by all appearances, wealthy Mexican American. He was living his dream.

———————————

Alex Macchi was enjoying the hunt. He was particularly enjoying the job for the Carrows family because he felt it was for a righteous cause. The job had all the elements of a "dream case," the theft of a valuable, historical gem, treachery, a betrayed beautiful woman, and a daughter abandoned. Finding David Torres was almost something he would do for free. He wanted him.

The Carrows family was also interesting, but he needed to know more about them. He had not met Charlotte in person but had spent some time watching her. He had to discover for himself what was happening with Julia's daughter. His experience with clients told him that they often didn't see the situation clearly. Not to mention those who told him outright lies for reasons of their own. He spent a couple of days following her and getting a feel for the life she and her daughter were living. After he had learned enough, he went to visit his parents at their home in the Bay Ridge area of Brooklyn.

"Momma," Alex said, hugging his mother, Marie. "It's so good to see you. I've missed you," he whispered in her ear tenderly. Pulling back, he saw tears forming in her eyes, which she immediately brushed away. She grabbed his hands and said, "Come in, come in, the boys and your father are ready to eat."

He held her hand as she led him into the spacious kitchen filled with the mouth-watering aromas of garlic and lemon. Alex looked at his family with deeply sentimental affection as he entered the room. His three brothers, Tony, Michael, and Nick, and his beloved father, Anthony Sr., rose when they saw him. They all greeted one another warmly, and Marie told them all to sit as she turned to get the plates on the table.

"Alexander," said his father, "you need to visit more often. You wouldn't believe what your mother cooked up for you. Alex's special dinner. We don't get her veal piccata unless Alexander comes home!"

"It's the latest thing," said Tony pouring from a bottle of Brunello. "Ma's using food to keep us coming round every Sunday. Each week is dedicated to someone special. Michael's special dinner, Nick's special dinner, Tony's special dinner, Isabella's special dinner. How can we pass on it?" he said good-naturedly.

"Like it's a big secret, me wanting my family around me as much as possible," said Marie, passing a plate to Alex.

"Where's Isabella?" said Alex, referring to his sister.

"She couldn't be here. She has parent-teacher conferences tonight. She was hoping you'd get a chance to see her tomorrow. How long will you be staying?" said his father.

"I'm not sure. Not long. I'm here on a case," he said, picking up his fork, ready to dive into the piccata.

"Put your fork down, Alex," said his mother. "We pray first. You take your turn tonight at the family table."

Alex, softened by the reminder, laid his fork down and cleared his throat. He'd been out of practice living alone in Los Angeles, away from all his family.

"Bless us, oh lord for these thy gifts, which we are about to receive from thy bounty. Through Christ our Lord, Amen. Oh, and on a personal note, thank you for the health of my loved ones and for my sainted mother's veal piccata. May she be allowed to share this gift with others when I am not present. Amen."

"Alex," his mother scolded, but she was barely heard as the men grabbed their forks and dove into their meals. Marie was grinning watching them take delight in her food and got up with a large linen dinner napkin and tucked it into Alex's shirt collar. He glanced at her adoringly while his brothers rolled their eyes.

"Tell us about the case you're working on," said Anthony Sr.

"You told me not to talk about the client's problems, Pop. You taught us that it's confidential, and we should never forget that they are trusting us with their secrets."

Anthony Sr. waved his hand. "That's for the office staff. Here in my home, among my family, your secrets are safe. We all understand this."

Alex had been teasing his father since the Macchi's were long in the habit of discussing his father's security and private detective cases with his family. They were a trusted team, and Alex's younger brother Michael had joined his father's firm of Macchi & Macchi some years before. Alex's oldest brother, Tony, was a police officer, and the youngest, Nick, was still in school but had expressed interest in joining the firm when he was through. It could be an exciting business.

"Where do I begin," Alex said with genuine concern. "There's a girl, a single mother, living in Manhattan whose mother has hired me to look into her circumstances. The family is very, *very* wealthy, but they cut her off after her boyfriend robbed them of an expensive jewel." Alex went into further detail but was careful not to reveal the family name.

He stopped to take a sip of the old Brunello and enjoyed the fig and chocolate flavors of the wine he was certain his mother had gone to great lengths to properly pair with the veal. He communicated a look of sincere appreciation toward her and continued, "Now, however, eighteen months after they cut her off, the *mother* is having regrets. She wants her family reunited, and she believes that if I can find the man who stole the jewel and bring him to her husband, that it will be an opening for reconciliation. They have miles to go in rebuilding their relationships, but I believe the mother is very determined to make it happen."

"She's a single mother, living alone in Manhattan without her family?" said Marie. "How does she support herself?" She poured more wine into Alex's glass.

"That's what I've been looking into while I'm here. I spent some time watching them over the last couple of days."

"What did you think of her? How does she seem to you?" said Marie.

Alex paused and looked away thoughtfully before he said, "She's really quite beautiful."

Anthony Sr. laid his fork on his plate and glancing briefly into his wife's smiling eyes, reached for the decanter of wine. "I see," he said. "Where did you see her?"

"I saw her arriving home, walking down the street in the West Village. She had on this kinda flowy pink dress that just moved as she walked," he said, trying unsuccessfully to describe the movement with his hands. "She seemed light, special. I had a picture of her, so I knew who I was looking for, but in person, it was like everyone around her was muted out, and she had this spotlight on her. She has a confidence and a strength but very feminine. Really, really pretty."

Unaware that everyone had stopped eating to listen to Alex's fanciful description as he was lost in thought describing the girl, Michael said, "A flowy pink dress. Huh. That'll get you every time."

"Alex, forget him," said Marie. "Have you seen her daughter? How old is she?"

"She's between three and four. The woman is doing well supporting them. She has a nice job in commercial real estate, and they seem to be doing fine. I watched her greet her daughter outside her front stoop when she got home from work. They both just lit up seeing each other. It was really moving. I get the feeling that they're very close. Later, I took a few pictures of the two of them. They were going to a dance studio, and the daughter had on a tutu and was carrying a bag, bouncing along. She looks exactly like her mother, and for that matter, her grandmother, the one who hired me. They were laughing. It was touching."

"Was she still wearing that flowy pink dress?" said Michael as he grabbed the bottle and was disappointed to find it empty.

Anthony Sr. waved his hand in Michael's direction and said, "She sounds special. I'm concerned that you've got some feelings for her, Alex. Is that wise? In a sense, she's your client."

"What? No! I've never even spoken to her," he said, startled.

"The way you're speaking about her, Alex," said Marie, getting up to get another bottle and handing it to Michael with a smile. "Usually it's *you* that gets in trouble with the clients. Being a white knight for them, protecting them, being a shoulder to cry on while you are helping them. It can be very seductive to women. And very dangerous for you. Although, I don't know how any woman would ever be able to resist you."

"We've come across this before," said Anthony Sr., "but your mother's right. You need to keep a professional distance," he counseled.

"Dad, please. I've never met her. I fully intend to keep my distance. I understand we have a professional responsibility."

"Like a doctor or a psychiatrist," said Marie, waving this off. "But, Alex, if there is something special, promise me you won't close your heart."

"Yeah, don't close your heart," said Nick, laughing.

"It's an interesting assignment," said Anthony Sr., trying to focus on the business aspect. "I can't believe the young thief got away with it. What took them so long to notice that the jewel was missing?"

"He swapped it with a replica. He worked at the Met and had access to a copy. I think it was just a happy coincidence for him, and he took advantage of it. I think he's an amateur and not a professional so he might not be as difficult to find. I have some leads I'm following up on. I just wanted to get the lay of the land here in New York. I needed to get an idea of how the woman and her daughter were doing so I could get a better understanding of the situation and make sure what my client told me lines up."

"If she's as beautiful as you say, why the hell did he leave her in the first place," said Nick loading his plate with seconds.

"People are complicated," said Anthony Sr. with a shrug. "Not everyone is motivated by the same thing. Money can be as powerful as beauty. The man couldn't have both, so he chose. It may be that simple."

"It will be my pleasure to find him. The family in California are very powerful people. I wonder what they'll do to him once I find him," Alex said with a small, satisfied smile.

Alarmed, his father said, "You don't think they'll harm him, do you? You're not the delivery boy for a hit?"

"No. No. I don't think they'd do that. In fact, I was worried about the same thing, but I can't imagine they'd do something to physically harm him. Possibly in other ways, but I think I'm okay with that."

"Retribution. An eye for an eye, a jewel for a jewel?" said Michael.

"We'll see. It should be interesting."

"Not to mention visually enjoyable," said Michael, baiting him.

But Alex was smiling again, lost in thought.

His mother Marie was beaming.

———————

Maybe it was because he saw Charlotte as a tragic victim or maybe because he found her life so compelling or maybe it was because she was so beautiful, but Alex had to admit that he had become more than intrigued by her. Watching her with Petunia and seeing how happy they were when they were together only made him want to protect them more.

Alex followed through with his leads from Sotheby's and did his research on the Tsarina's Fancy. He tracked down everyone who had bid on the ring. One gentleman, in particular, caught his attention. A Mr. Victor Al Nahyan from Dubai. Alex called Julia to inform her of his progress.

"Julia, I believe I have a solid lead on the buyer of the jewel. A Mr. Victor Al Nahyan in Dubai was an active bidder for the ring the day of the auction and as we know was ultimately outbid by Henry. But in addition to that, I found out that Mr. Al Nahyan was a major patron of the Romanov Jewels traveling exhibition and the primary reason it was allowed to be featured at the Burj Al Arab Jumeirah in Dubai. A man who would bid on the stone at auction and lose it to someone else and would later support an exhibit of the Tsar's jewelry has more than a passing interest. He might be the most interested buyer for the jewel. In fact, when the exhibition left Dubai, its next stop was New York City. He may have met David at the Met at that time. I think it's worthwhile to find out."

"I agree," she said. "That sounds very promising."

"I'm in New York now and have attempted to learn a little something about your daughter and her routines before I ultimately approach her. I took the liberty of forwarding a few pictures of her and Petunia to you. I'll be in touch as soon as I know if Mr. Al Nahyan leads me to David."

"Thank you, Alex. I appreciate it."

After speaking with Alex, Julia rushed to her computer and pulled up the pictures. She stared at her beautiful daughter and granddaughter and wept for all they had lost.

Chapter 12

Alex made the flight from New York to Dubai with a layover in Amsterdam in about twenty hours, and he checked into the Burj Al Arab Jumeirah. He knew very little about Victor Al Nahyan but hoped the man was in the city.

Concierges were similar creatures the world over. They exceled in accommodating not only their guests but by extension, everyone they came in contact with. The more people and more connections they had, the better they were at their jobs and the better the tips. Alex and the concierge at the Burj Al Arab were similar because both of their jobs depended upon discretion. When Alex met a young, cultured concierge named Kayani, he knew they would be able to come to an understanding.

What Alex knew about Victor was that he was a benefactor of the museum located in the hotel. And the museum would know some of the basic details of his life and how to contact him as well. He assured Kayani that he only wanted a respectful introduction to Victor Al Nahyan. He needed to have a brief conversation with him, and he reassured Kayani that in no way would the conversation lead to any harm to Victor. With the fortune of the Carrows family at his disposal courtesy of Julia Carrows, Alex's budget was extensive. He presented Kayani with an impressively motivating tip.

Kayani was cooperative and knew a meeting could be arranged. He actually knew Mr. Al Nahyan through the museum in the hotel and also through his very close relationship with the proprietor of the museum. A meeting was arranged between the American and Victor Al Nahyan to take place several days later in one of the world-class restaurants at the hotel.

That evening Mr. Victor Al Nahyan was seated comfortably in the Skyview Bar at a table for two with views overlooking the Persian Gulf and the city of Dubai. He was alone, waiting with interest for the appointment with the mysterious American who purportedly had a personal favor to ask of him. When Alex approached, Victor realized he had never met the gentleman.

Alex extended his hand. "Mr. Al Nahyan, I greatly appreciate you taking the time to meet with me this evening. My name is Alex Macchi."

Victor was pleased and slightly relieved upon meeting the American, that he was impeccably dressed, respectably polished, and not someone who appeared threatening.

"Please have a seat, Mr. Macchi. Would you care for a drink before we conduct our business?"

"Yes," he said as the waiter approached. Alex's eyes drifted to Victor's glass filled with a deep-colored red wine.

Victor waved toward it and said, "Sangiovese. Exceptional."

"I'll have the same," Alex said to the waiter.

"Thank you again for taking time out of your schedule to meet with me, Mr. Al Nahyan. I can assure you that our business will be brief this evening, and I won't take up any more of your time than necessary. In addition, I can promise you that what I need to ask you will be in confidence and will only lend to helping a great many people."

Mr. Al Nahyan was curious about what Mr. Macchi would have to say. He seemed to be cordial and sincere, but Victor was naturally wary.

"I would like to tell you a story," Alex began. "I represent a woman whose daughter and family have been cruelly shamed and wildly taken advantage of by a man you may know. After I finish telling you this story, my favor of you is to give me the location of this man. After that, I will leave, and you have my word, my assurance, that no consequence will come your way."

"I'm not sure if I can help you, Mr. Macchi, but I'm interested in this story. Please continue." Victor relaxed and took a sip of his wine.

"My client has a daughter living in New York City who was dating a man whom she met in college. They fell in love, and after some time, the daughter brought the boy with her to the family home for an introduction. One night, the boy secretly robbed the family of a precious family heirloom and then in a letter dumped the girl without looking back. He abandoned her. In addition, she was pregnant with this man's child. The family felt shame and horror at what happened and blamed the daughter for her lack of awareness of this man's true character and have since also abandoned her and her child."

Alex reached into his breast pocket and pulled out an up-close picture of lovely Charlotte and beautiful Petunia smiling into each other's eyes. He handed it to Victor.

"This is a picture of the girl and her daughter. The mother of the family hired me to find the man who started a vicious avalanche of repercussions, which fell on the heels of his actions." Alex paused the story and looked at Victor with hopeful compassion.

"I believe you know who the father is and where he can be found, Mr. Al Nahyan. The mother of the family only wants to repair the damage that has been done to her family. She wants to hold her daughter and granddaughter and bring healing and peace back into their home."

Victor looked at Alex and shook his head. "I'm not sure how I would possibly know who this man is. I don't know the woman or child in this photograph."

"I believe you do. And once again, I want to strongly assure you that in no way will any harm come to you for helping me find him. My job and reputation are based on diplomatic solutions for my clients and those whom I encounter along the way."

"Mr. Macchi, I will try to help you if I can. What was the boy's name?" he said, piqued.

"David Torres."

Victor sat back and stared at Alex Macchi with what he hoped conveyed a look of innocence. Of course. This was about the ring. An inquiry was something he expected might one day happen but not presented in this fashion, and not after so many years.

"I'm afraid you've wasted your time. I don't know a man named David Torres," he said and placed the picture on the table.

Alex bowed his head and took a breath and then politely resumed. "Victor, I'm afraid that you do. I believe you met Mr. Torres in New York City through the Metropolitan Museum of Art. Specifically through the traveling exhibition known as the Romanov Jewels, which you accompanied from Dubai to Manhattan. I believe Mr. Torres came to you after switching the fake Tsarina's Fancy for the real one in the home of Mr. Henry Carrows." He nodded his head toward the picture. "That is his daughter, Charlotte, and his only granddaughter, Petunia."

Although Mr. Al Nahyan obviously knew David Torres, he was shocked by this turn of events and the family tragedy that unfolded after David sold the stone to him. He hadn't cared about Mr. Henry Carrows and the loss of his jewel, but as a father of daughters himself, he now felt something more personal about this girl and her daughter. It was intriguing to own such information. He had no idea the family had suffered such internal strife after the theft.

Alex watched Mr. Al Nahyan process the information. He continued, "In a perfect world, the Carrows would like the diamond back, but even more than that," he impressed, "they want to settle with David. Help us track David, and they will never pursue the diamond. That you purchased it from David Torres was troubling news to them, but they've had almost two years of suffering since they uncovered that a switch had been made.

"Mr. Henry Carrows is a private man, and Julia Carrows, Charlotte's mother, is only trying to reunite her family. Mr. Carrows is only interested in David, the former boyfriend of his daughter, the father of his only grandchild, and the only person in his eyes who needs to be settled with. You have the assurance of the Carrows family that they will not pursue you or any buyer and current owner of the Tsarina's Fancy. They only want David."

Victor picked up the picture, examining it again, and handed it back to Alex with a small, satisfied smile. He sat back and turned a gold ring on his finger, cocking his head in consideration and said, "I like to think of Henry Carrows in discomfort. It gives me satisfaction to think of him discovering that he has been tricked. He is quite a trickster himself. Did you know that?"

Alex didn't respond but waited.

Victor shrugged. "But the family tragedy is something new. It's difficult to think of Henry Carrows having feelings, but I suppose since he is a father he must have a beating heart."

Alex gently placed the picture back in front of Victor again and said, "I can assure you that he does, Mr. Al Nahyan. They need each other. Are you a father?"

"I am," he said proudly. "I have many children."

"You're a very lucky man. I wish them all good health. Won't you help these women? Julia Carrows misses her daughter and granddaughter. They've all struggled incredibly since David Torres betrayed them. No one is blaming you for taking advantage of an opportunity. No one wants to blame you. Or look for you. We're only interested in David. I need to find him, and I know you can help me."

Alex sat back and watched as Victor drained the contents of his glass.

"In fact, I think you want to help them, Mr. Al Nahyan," Alex pressed. "I think you know it's the right thing to do. You're a father. You know what it feels like to see one of your children suffer. Every parent does. You can help them. You're a successful businessman. You won here. You got what you wanted, you got the ring. You bought it. It's yours."

Alex pressed. "One lead. One direction. Point me to him. Please. I promise you we'll leave in peace if you help us find him."

Victor smiled broadly and said, "Are you enjoying your Sangiovese? It was good, but I feel like something bolder. Tell me. Have you been to Roberto's? It is a favorite of mine in the city. They have a table there," he said putting his hand on his heart, his eyes wide in disbelief, "in *my* name! Anytime I want, they welcome me home. The food. Ahhh. Exquisite. The scenery, ah. And I happen to know that they have an excellent selection of Amarone."

Victor leaned in, his eyebrows raised with enthusiasm. "Perhaps we should discuss your situation further. Over dinner?"

Alex retrieved the picture of Charlotte and Petunia and put it in his jacket pocket. He gave a knowing smile to Mr. Al Nahyan and said, "I'd be delighted. And I insist that you be my guest."

Victor threw his head back and laughed loudly. "But of course! I wouldn't have it any other way."

As they left the Burj Al Arab, the hot air hit their faces as they walked into the night. Victor regaled Alex, enthusiastically describing the meal they were about to have and the exciting opportunities for nighttime adventure in his city.

———————

Alex woke the next morning with mixed emotions. His first was relief that he had made it back to his hotel respectfully, making it through the lobby to his room in one piece with most of his memory intact. His head was killing him, the luxurious surroundings in his room spinning. He closed his eyes and tried to recall the evening.

Amarone. God, 14 percent alcohol. He couldn't believe how much Victor had drunk. The tannins were killing him. He slowly sat up and made his way to the bathroom for some aspirin and a glass of water. What a night. The burly Victor might have been one of the nicest men he had ever known. His level of joy for nearly all of his passions was impossible to resist. His capacities for everything were enormous. It was no wonder they had a table in his name at Robertos. From the moment they entered until the moment they left, Victor's arm hooked through Alex's, the man was larger than life. A big, gregarious force whose bear hug with Alex at the end of the night was physically painful.

Alex looked at his pitiful form in the mirror and couldn't help smiling as he remembered the most important part. "David Torres *Cordoza*. São Paulo, Brazil. I'm coming for you, man."

He stumbled back to bed, relieved that Los Angeles was eleven hours behind him. He couldn't decently call Julia Carrows with the good news until 9:00 p.m. Dubai time. He sincerely hoped he'd feel better by then.

Julia grabbed the phone, wildly anxious that morning when Alex called.

"Mrs. Carrows. Good morning, how are you?"

"Mr. Macchi," she said, trying to stay calm. "I've been waiting for your call. I hope you have good news from your meeting?" she said.

"I do. I have good news," he said.

Julia breathed a sigh of relief.

"I know what happened to the ring."

"Oh, my god."

"Julia," he said and stopped. "May I call you that?"

"Yes, of course you can, Alex," she said impatiently. "What did you find out?"

"I'll tell you everything, but before I begin, before I tell you what I learned, I'm wondering if I can secure a promise from you. Without your permission, I made a guarantee to the man who purchased the ring that neither you nor Henry would seek retrieval of it or retaliate against him in any way for purchasing it. I gave him my word as your representative that in no way would you seek either legal or personal vengeance against him. For that, he was willing to reveal the whereabouts of David Torres.

"May I have your word on that promise before proceeding, Julia?" he said cautiously.

Julia was uncertain and slightly unsettled that Alex had negotiated this with the stranger who now had illegal possession of their property. She was uncertain that Henry would feel magnanimous toward the receiver of their stolen goods. But she had had enough. No amount of money was worth the price of her family. She didn't care about the Arab man that had purchased it. She only cared about finding David and bringing him to Henry. She also knew that when Henry found out about this investigation, she would need to use all her ability to persuade him to focus on David and keep the promise that she was about to make to Alex.

"You have my word. Where is he?"

"São Paulo, Brazil," he said.

Chapter 13

David Cordoza, São Paulo, Brazil. Not much to go on in a city of eleven million people. But in a world with computers and Facebook, the search would be easier. Alex didn't think David would be brazen enough to set up a social profile with pictures on the internet, but if he was living a public lifestyle in the art communities in São Paulo or even Rio de Janeiro, then he could be found. But Alex also knew that his information from Mr. Al Nahyan was over four years old. Anything could have happened to David during that time.

Flights from Dubai to São Paulo, Brazil, were about twenty-three hours, again with a layover in Amsterdam. Alex knew he needed to put eyes directly on David before he could bring Charlotte into the picture. He needed to find David and discover as much as he could about him, his home, and lifestyle before it was decided how they could convince him to return to the United States.

Julia had been kind enough to encourage Alex, possibly as a reward for finding the latest link in the chain of events, to fly business class. After the flight was over, Alex felt that the $5,000 upgrade had been worth every penny. He was grateful for the time and space he had had to plan and consider his next move.

He spent his time poring over the background of the city and the museum, art, and nightlife crowd. Unfortunately, he didn't get lucky and stumble across a picture of David, but he had a broad idea of how he should begin. Also, unfortunately, Alex spoke no Portuguese and only some Spanish. Being from Brooklyn and from Italian heritage, he had some conversational ability in Italian. With Spanish being a sister romance language, he could hack his way through a short conversation in Spanish, but not effectively. And of course, Spanish was not exactly Portuguese. He realized the language barrier would slow him down. He was going to require some local help.

The law firm he was loosely affiliated with in Los Angeles, Baach, McKenzie & Blake, had a large number of employees fluent in Spanish. It could be an option to get one of his associates on a plane to São Paolo. They could be counted on for discretion as well. But would they blend in or would the two of them stick out like the lost Americans they were? After taking a mental inventory of his options at the firm, he decided that he would need help hired locally.

He did reach out to the firm, however, for a recommendation on a reliable source.

"I'm going to need someone in a sister capacity over here who would be willing to help me find this man and who would keep his mouth shut," he explained to a senior partner at the firm.

"We have business dealings and a relationship with a firm in São Paulo. It's a large partnership firm founded in

New York with offices in London, Hong Kong, Caymans, São Paulo, and a few others. JLC Piper. They handle international law, copyright, litigation, banking, and criminal law, pretty much everything. The name of the guy there you could call is Pedro Keener. I believe he can be trusted with your inquiries. It goes without saying that you may lend our name to them. Let me know what happens, Alex," he said as they said goodbye.

Pedro Keener took the call immediately when Alex said he was an associate of Baach, McKenzie & Blake in LA. Pedro, fluent in English, listened carefully as Alex explained.

"I've just arrived in São Paolo, and unfortunately, I don't speak Portuguese. I have a client in the States who is searching for a relative whom they believe may have had some connections in São Paolo or Rio. The family is quite anxious to find the man and to let him know that his mother is dying. They're very private people, and I would need assistance from someone who would be discreet and who has a level of sophistication to find him. Do you have anyone in São Paolo whom you think would be of use to our firm and me?"

Within the hour, Pedro got back to him with a name.

Alex had checked into the InterContinental São Paulo in the Jardins neighborhood, primarily because it was near the Museum of Art of São Paulo. He expected to spend some time there getting to know the museums in the area. Mr. Miguel Ríos met him in his suite the next day.

Alex was uncertain how much he should share with Miguel. The entire truth was out of the question. The truth that he had broadly outlined to Miguel's partner at the law firm would be a start, and he would take it from there.

"Mr. Alex Macchi?" Miguel said by way of introduction as he held out his hand.

"Yes, Mr. Ríos, please come in," Alex said as he escorted him into the suite. "Do you mind if I call you Miguel?"

"No, please do, and you are Alex?"

"Yes. Thank you for coming. Have a seat. Mr. Keener was very quick with my special request for a partner and interpreter while I'm in São Paolo. Did he tell you anything about the business I'll be conducting here?" Alex said as he took a seat across from him.

"Only that you work for Baach, McKenzie & Blake out of Los Angeles and that you're searching for someone on a client's behalf in São Paolo."

"That is partially correct. I am searching for a man who I believe may live in São Paolo, but I am only loosely associated with the law firm. I conduct for them their more discreet investigations for their clients. I might be considered a private investigator if that would be the term here?"

"Yes, an *investigador particular.*" Miguel nodded.

"You speak English beautifully. Are you originally from São Paolo?"

"Yes, originally, but my father is from the United States, so we always spoke English and Portuguese in my home growing up. And I've been to the US many times on business and on family occasions."

"So, are you an *investigador particular* or an attorney at JLC Piper?" Alex questioned.

"I'm both actually. I think I might be a fellow colleague in the field of discreet inquiries. That is a capacity in which I find myself most of the time, as I think I have found I am suited to the business," he said, smiling pleasantly.

Introductions aside, they relaxed as Alex began to explain the situation.

"I told Mr. Keener that I'm searching for a man who went missing several years ago. We have reason to believe that he came to São Paulo with the intent of making a home either here or in Rio. When he left, the man, unfortunately, abandoned his family and his young child. I have been asked by the family to find him, as the mother of the family is now dying, and she would like to see him again before she passes away."

"What do you know about him here in São Paolo?" Miguel said politely.

"I know nothing of his activities in the city. I only have his name, his age, his photograph, and an idea of what he might be doing to support himself," Alex said, considering.

"Well, that is a good start. Especially what he does for a living. If he is a laborer or something transient, then that would pose a problem. But if he does something more specific, a certain profession or field, that would be more helpful. Why don't you give me the details on what you do know?" Miguel said, tossing his hands in the air.

Alex nodded. "I agree, it's a start, but before I begin, I need to receive assurances that you will not share the details of our search with any other parties. Including Mr. Keener. My clients require this confidentiality for personal reasons."

Miguel scratched his head thoughtfully and shrugged. "I give you my word as an attorney in the state of Brazil, as well as my word as a man and fellow colleague. Our work will be private and kept that way. It is what we do, is it not?" He smiled knowingly.

"Yes, it certainly is," Alex said, returning the smile. "Let's begin."

Alex reached into his bag and pulled out a picture of David that he had obtained from his passport. He handed it to Miguel. "His name is David Cordoza. This photo is six years old. He was born in the United States in Inglewood, California. He attended school at NYU in New York City where he studied art history. He worked at the Metropolitan Museum of Art for four years during which time he was an assistant curator of the exhibitions department. While working at the Met, he left suddenly and has not been seen or heard from since. He sent a note to his parents explaining his reasons for leaving, but I won't share those with you just now. I very strongly believe he would be working in some capacity in the art world. I also believe he is well polished, trilingual in Spanish, English, and Portuguese, lives well, and is probably successful. In addition, he would also dress well to foster that appearance. He would need that to rub shoulders with the moneyed and artistic patrons of the city. He is ambitious."

It was enough. Miguel knew where to begin.

Alex had learned that Miguel Ríos was a Paulistano. Born in the city of São Paulo, raised by a family with means, and formally educated with a degree in law, he was the ideal candidate as a partner to Alex. JLC Piper was a strong supporter and patron of the São Paulo Corinthians soccer team as well as the Museum of Art. Miguel had attended functions at this museum in particular and had visited most of the others over the course of his lifetime.

Alex couldn't decide if he wanted to flash David's picture around the museum. How would that appear, and could it get back to David that someone was looking for him? Alex knew they would need some plausible reason to be looking for him.

Miguel suggested they first reach out to the events coordinator at the museum and simply ask her if she knew the man. Miguel got her name from the administrator at the firm who was in charge of event planning and fundraisers.

Miguel picked up his phone and said in Portuguese, "Hello, I'm calling from JLC Piper and was wondering if you could help me locate a man my boss came into contact with at our last fundraiser? He was describing a piece of art my boss was interested in buying, but then he lost the man's phone number. He remembered his name is David Cordoza? Would you happen to know him?"

"I'm on hold," Miguel whispered to Alex. "She wanted to ask a couple of people down the hall who had stepped out."

Miguel's attention went back to the phone. "Yes? I see, okay thank you for your help. Bye."

"Alex, they know of him," he said with excitement. "If it's the right person, they believe he works primarily for the Paulo Institute, but they aren't completely sure. Pull up the website, and let's take a look."

The Paulo Institute's website did not contain pictures but listed as a patron was the name David Cordoza.

"What now? Should we call them?" Miguel said with restrained excitement.

"I think we should," said Alex.

"But what if he's there, and they try to connect him to me?" Miguel said with concern.

"Just hang up. If he's not there, ask them if he has a direct phone line. That will indicate whether he has an office in the building. If they say no and give you his cell, just take it. But before they try to connect you or give you his number, find out who the person is to speak to regarding upcoming fundraisers for the institute."

"Okay," Miguel said as he began dialing. "Hello? Yes, I was wondering if I may speak with a Mr. David Cordoza. I see," Miguel said with confidence. "I know he's a patron of the museum, and I was wondering how to get a hold of him regarding a fundraiser?" Miguel listened. "No, you don't need to connect me. I've got it. You've been very helpful. Thank you!"

Miguel hung up, clapped his hands quickly, and shook them out. "Well, Alex, we are batting a thousand! No, they had no number for him, but they wanted to know if I wanted to speak with a Barbara, who is in charge of the fundraising for the museum. I told her no, because, Alex, she also mentioned that he would probably be at the event they're holding tomorrow night at the museum celebrating its first one hundred years."

Alex smiled like a Cheshire cat. It was coming together.

The next evening, Miguel Ríos would represent the firm of JLC Piper at the One-Hundredth Anniversary Gala at the Paulo Institute. He'd memorized David Cordoza's face and spent the evening socializing while searching for him. And it paid off. They found him.

Miguel texted Alex with the news and a picture he had taken in the general vicinity of David. Alex texted him back, "Good work, Miguel. Keep an eye on him, and text me when you see him leaving. I'll pick up his track outside the museum, then you leave as well. We'll double team our trail in case he doesn't go straight home, or go home at all."

Which is exactly what they did.

David Cordoza was still young and handsome but had grown into his looks as a man. He had also developed a countenance of supreme and easygoing confidence, which Alex wondered if he had possessed when he left New York City or if he had developed it over time. Over the course of the next few days, Miguel and Alex researched and watched David maneuver through his life. He had purchased an apartment in the Jardins neighborhood, not far from Alex's hotel. They knew he had patronage at several museums across the city and was primarily in a position at those museums to keep the money flowing in. He did this with apparent success. During the time Alex followed David in São Paulo, he did not see any particular lady accompany him or visit him in his apartment. Miguel approached the concierge of David's apartment building, but the man was unsure if there was a girlfriend in the picture. He reported that there was definitely no Mrs. Cordoza or children. David appeared to be single.

———

Alex met Miguel for the last time in the lobby of his hotel.

"Thanks for everything. You've been a big help. I know the family will really appreciate it," Alex said, handing him an envelope of cash.

Miguel tucked it into his jacket and looked at Alex with suspicion. "You're not going to tell David that his poor mother is dying? Bring him back to the States with you, Alex?"

"No. Not right now," he said simply, meeting his eye contact.

"So, I'm guessing you want more from David than you're letting on," said Miguel with a small grin.

Alex smiled and shook his friend's hand. "You're very good at your job, Miguel. I wouldn't have expected anything less. I appreciate your discretion, of course."

"Of course. I'm curious what's behind all this, but I know better than to ask the question. Let me know if you need any help in the future, Alex. It was a pleasure getting to know you."

———————————

Alex called Julia. He was going to New York to see Charlotte. It was time for Julia to give her a call.

Chapter 14

Charlotte was weary after another long but successful day in heels working at Ramsey Towers. She loved having a job where she could blend her highly attuned intuitive skills and her multilayered background. She could mold herself into whatever type of person was needed to close the deal, pulling from her experiences raised in a wealthy lifestyle, the belief in the art of seduction, her education, and her kickass wardrobe. She was an actor, walking onto the set each day, merging onto the path of circumstances her clients presented and putting her finger on the precise button that would win them over.

It was Sun Tzu that said you must appear weak when you are strong and strong when you are weak, but it was her father who taught the importance of the precept. Now that she hadn't heard from her mother or father in over eighteen months, she was pulling mighty hard on the latter half of the proverb. It still amazed her that not only had they cut her off financially, but they had also cut her off from their lives. Maybe she shouldn't have been so surprised. She hadn't reached out to them either. It was a painful stalemate that she tried very hard not to care about. Instead, she focused on the positive. Since she'd been cut off, she'd built a good life for her and Petunia. They were doing very well.

She often thought of the last phone call with her mom and came close to calling home many times but had always held back. She was still too angry. She made a number of decisions immediately after they cut her off, the first of which was that she wanted to retain her home. She knew she could have made a fortune on the sale of the town-home, but she didn't want to sell it. It was her home. And, it was the only one Petunia knew.

Instead, she decided to get a job and get a tenant. She succeeded in obtaining both. Between the success of the job at Frank and Son and her income that she received from James, they were doing just fine. James rented the garden level of her home, which she had rarely used. It was more of a studio, but it had a small kitchen, full bath, and a washer and dryer. Her neighborhood in the West Village was almost exclusively made up of families, and Charlotte could afford to ask a lot of money for the apartment. But she needed someone she could tolerate and trust, for though they would have separate entrances, they would be in constant proximity to each other. She had posted an ad on campus, and she couldn't believe her luck when James applied. He had some money, and while working on his dissertation, he wanted to live in a quiet neighborhood close to campus. It was a great match for both of them. Charlotte would drop Petunia off at school or daycare first thing in the morning, and James would take care of her in the afternoons. The three of them had a nice peaceful routine.

Walking now toward her home, shaking off the day, her regrets, and her memories, she saw James sitting by himself on the stoop of her home.

"Hi, James! Where's Pinky?"

"She just ran inside for a cookie. We were waiting for you on the stoop. You know she loves to do the people-watching thing from her 'stoopy,'" he said with amusement.

Just then, Petunia came outside with two cookies, saw her mom, and ran to her, arms outstretched, a cookie in each hand.

"Mommy! You're home! I have cookies! These have the most chips," she said as she gave a cookie to James. Charlotte could see her contemplating what to do with the other one. She squinted up at her and said tentatively, "Do you want a cookie?"

"No, honey, that one's all for you. Thank you for the offer though." She smiled and patted her on the head.

Petunia gave a smile of relief, sat down close to James, and began to eat the treat.

"How was your day?" Charlotte asked.

Petunia squished up her face, her mouth full of cookie and garbled out, "Eh wa phuunnn."

"That's very good to hear. James, how was your day?" she said, smiling broadly.

James put the last of his cookie in his mouth and imitated Petunia, "It was phunnnn too."

Petunia got the joke and started laughing, holding her mouth full of cookie closed with her tiny hands. They all laughed, and it delighted Charlotte to see her daughter so happy. She reached out and extended her hand. "Well, I had a phunn day, too. What do you say we go inside and get ready for dinner? What do you think? James, you interested in some spaghetti later or are you all full from the cookies?"

"I'm all full from the cookies. But thanks. Another time," he said rising and walking down the stairs. "See you later, Pinky." He waved.

Petunia waved happily back in his direction. "Bye, James!"

Charlotte reached down and picked her up. Petunia put her arms around her neck, and Charlotte gave her a kiss on the cheek before opening the door to their home.

———————

That evening after Charlotte had put Petunia down for the night, she went downstairs to the kitchen and put her daughter's pink backpack onto the kitchen counter. She went through it, inspecting the contents for a wayward smashed cracker, wet sock, or treasured piece of artwork that came home from the preschool on a regular basis. The creative crafts were getting more sophisticated as she got older. They did a wonderful job supplying the kids with cool projects. Today, it was the top of a can of frozen juice with Pinky's smiling face glued onto the middle. Colored sequins were glued haphazardly around the rim, and there was a magnet on the backside. It was a thing of beauty.

Charlotte smiled, walked to the refrigerator, and placed it near another treasure. She loved it.

Just then, her cell phone rang. She was shocked when she saw the number. It was her mother. She answered the phone.

"Hello?" she said, unsettled.

"Hi, Charlotte, it's Mom."

"Hi, Mom," Charlotte said cautiously.

"I was calling to see how you are doing?" Julia asked casually.

"How am I doing? I'm doing great! Things are really good here. How are you?" she said with an awkward tension, unsure of what else to say.

"We're fine. Your dad's good. He's been staying downtown the last week while he's working on something since he just hates the commute. You know how he is with traffic. No patience at all."

"That's true. No patience at all. How is everyone else, Charles and Carey?" she said, taking a small step, uncertain where this was going.

"They're fine too. How is Petunia?" she said with real emotion.

Charlotte relaxed slightly, eager to share moments about her sweet child. "I just put her down. She's amazing," she said, glancing briefly back at the new picture on the fridge. "I think she grows every day. She's so beautiful. It's interesting to see that her face is getting freckles. She's taking dance classes, and I guess it won't be a surprise to you, but she's got some natural skill. Her teachers think she's really coordinated for her age. Combine that with her big personality, it might make her a standout. I'm not ruling anything else out, but if I had to guess, I think she's found her sport."

"I miss her. I miss you too, Charlotte," Julia said in a shaky, emotional voice.

Charlotte didn't know what to think about this call out of the blue. She also didn't know what to feel. Right now, she felt guarded. She didn't want to be hurt again. She walked over to the backpack and placed her hand gently on her daughter's things.

"I miss you too, Mom," she said, although she wasn't sure at that moment if she did.

"Why are you calling, Mom? Is something else going on?" she said with suspicion.

"Well, yes, there is something going on that I wanted to speak to you about."

"Okay, what is it?" she said with an edge.

"I want you to listen to me. All the way. All the way through about what I need to tell you. Please don't hang up or anything, okay?"

Oh god. What? She sat down on a barstool and got ready.

"Okay," Charlotte said with a grimace.

"Some months ago, I hired a private detective to find David," Julia said flatly.

"What!? You did what?" Charlotte yelled, jumping up.

"Charlotte! Please let me finish! Please let me explain. I did it because I love you. And I love my granddaughter, and we were wrong to punish you when we discovered the ring was missing. I didn't think it would destroy our family, but it's done that because you're not here. We don't see you. No one has any intention of seeing each other! It's now this horrible stalemate, and I want it to END." Julia was crying openly now.

Oh, my god. Her mother was crying. Charlotte couldn't remember the last time her mother had cried. And she was crying over their breakup? She wanted to believe it, but she didn't trust it.

"What are you saying, Mom? Did the detective find him? Does Dad know about this?" she said, shocked.

Recovering herself, she said, "No, your dad does not know about this. I did this myself. I don't want the family to be permanently fractured, and you know it's headed in that direction. I need to stop it. And I wasn't sure how, but over the last year I decided that if your father could confront David directly, then maybe he would let go of some of his bitterness, and the two of you could find your way back to at least being civil."

"So, Dad doesn't know anything about this?" She began to angrily pace the kitchen. "He isn't interested in apologizing to me or reaching out, is that correct?"

"Okay, I know you're angry. I know he is not a perfect person, but I also know the toll this has taken on him. And also on me. I very rarely take a stand when it comes to that man, but I am now. I'm sorry it's taken me so long. I should have stopped this madness months ago."

Charlotte was floored by this belated observation. Her eyes wide, shaking her head, she blurted out in frustration, "You should have stepped in a million times, Mom. Where were you when that monster of a sister was cutting my face out of all the family pictures? Where were you when she lied to my boyfriend that I had VD? Where were you when she and Charles stole that lady's handbag and put it in my room? God! There were a million times you were never there for me!" she shouted.

Julia took it. She was listening, finally. "I know, I know, I know, you are right. There were so many times I should have stepped in and corralled her and your brother, and your father for that matter, but I just didn't! I don't know, it wasn't in my nature. I didn't want to interfere with any of your father's decisions, and he felt that most of his decisions were right. But I should have. I should have. I know that now. Seeing Petunia born was one of the greatest moments of my life, and I let it go, I let it all go, all the love and our relationship when I followed Henry's lead again after he found out he'd been robbed.

"I didn't know what to do, Charlotte! He was hysterical. I couldn't defy him, not then. I just didn't have any practice at that. I wanted to, but I didn't. And I'm sorry. Because after the dust settled, I looked around and realized that you were never going to come back. That I had lost you and Petunia too. And that was just too much. I realized you would use all those strengths that you've been given and marshal them against us. I realized that your strength would keep you from ever reaching out. I knew you could manage without us, but I knew I could never manage without you."

There was a heavy pause. Julia, sniffing slightly, her tone softer said, "You've inherited your father's stubborn nature, Charlotte. The two of you have been arguing your entire lives. I just tried to stay out of the way. I thought you should work through your problems together. I always imagined you could work it out as you got older. That the two of you would find your way."

Charlotte left the kitchen and walked downstairs to the living room. She realized she needed to put more distance between herself and her daughter still hopefully sleeping upstairs. "But silence matters, Mom. Your silence. You're my mom. I needed someone to help me and listen to me, to understand me, and there wasn't anyone willing to be supportive. Dad was so busy being this big king, this master of the universe, he never listened to me or believed in the things I was saying. He tried to make me think that there was something wrong with me. That my sensitivities, my feelings about things were wrong. To be ashamed of my heart. When it was breaking, it was wrong. When I felt too much love, it was wrong. Everything I did was wrong. He kept saying that everyone else in the house got along just fine, and it was me, only me that had a problem.

"But I wasn't a problem! I shouldn't have been *a problem*! I should have been listened to and respected for who I was. Why was that so difficult to understand? Why the constant scolding, everyone trying to change my personality? I mean, how can you ask someone to change their nature? Why would you do that? Why didn't you and Dad just love me for who I was?"

"Did you feel love, Charlotte? Did you know that we loved you?" Julia questioned forcefully.

"Mom," she said, stumbling, uncertain she even wanted to say it, "yes. Somewhere, inside me, I knew that you loved me. All of you, but it wasn't enough. I couldn't breathe right when I was around Dad, around you, around Charles or Carey. My god, why are you all so blind to *their* faults? Carey is a terrible person. She's said so many hateful things to me, just to see me hurt! Who does that? Why did she need to hurt me all the time, and why in the name of god was that behavior tolerated, and mine wasn't? Words matter, Mom. They're weapons, and she used them against me all the time. But it was always my fault! Always me, not shaking it off, standing up to her, being stronger, always insisting that there was something wrong with me.

"And Charles, he laughed. Always laughing. When he saw some of the shit go down, he was always there with the jokes. Carey listens to him. Always has. In fact, I saw him stand up to Carey a couple of times. It was amazing how much she responded. I loved him for those moments. You have no idea how much I wanted to worship him too. My big brother. He was my champion, sometimes, not you, not Dad. But I also remember his glee. He enjoyed the show."

"I should have stopped them. I know that now. I didn't see everything that you're accusing them of, but there were times, I thought I stepped in? Didn't I?" Julia asked hopefully.

"Honestly, I can't remember much of that. I went to you, I wrote you letters, do you remember that?" Charlotte said, nearly exhausted, closing her eyes.

"I do. They were so dark, you seemed so unhappy. I didn't know what to do. I thought we were giving you a beautiful life. You had so much! I didn't have the advantages you had as a child, and I didn't think it was correct to indulge what I saw was an ungratefulness."

"Money isn't the issue, Mom!" she said throwing her arm up in exasperation. "That's just the scenery! Stuff! The issue was the family, the love, the hurt, the pain, who we are as human beings. Who I was and who you wanted me to be. I needed to get out of there because no one ever supported me."

"That's just not true, Charlotte. We did support you. We encouraged you. We all loved you."

She slumped onto a sofa and put her head in her hand, trying to regain her composure. "Okay, let's say that's true. Because I know on some level it's got to be true. But for me, it was just too much. I was too hurt and damaged, and I needed to find out for myself to see if there was really something wrong with me. If Dad was right, and I should change the way I am."

"And what have you discovered?" Julia questioned.

"I discovered that there's nothing wrong with me, Mom," she said, her voice dropping. "Not fundamentally. But I still carry the wounds, and I still have a family that doesn't understand who I am. But I do know now that you love me. Because I'm a mom now too. Petunia is my world. I know as a mother that you will always love me because I can't imagine it any other way."

"Your father loves you just as much as I do, Charlotte. He feels pain too, he just doesn't show it. He misses you more than he's willing to admit, he just hasn't known how to express it and fix the hole he dug for the two of you," she said with regret.

"I don't know how to help him. I've told him how I feel a million times, but he won't listen to me." Her eyes traveled over to a book on a high shelf that she knew contained photographs of her family. She'd been afraid to bring it down in case Petunia saw it and started asking questions.

"I think he's willing to listen, honey. Maybe he wasn't willing to listen when you were younger, I'll agree with you, but now, especially with his granddaughter out there in the world and him not having a relationship with her, it hurts and confuses him greatly. I'm trying, I'm *going* to make this right," she said with conviction.

"I promise you if you'll meet me halfway, if you'll trust me, together we can fix this. I want us to be a family again, Charlotte. Please, we need to see you. I want to hold you and Petunia. Your father needs you in his arms too. He wants to meet his granddaughter. I'm sorry for the pain that you went through, and I'm apologizing for not helping you when you needed the help, my understanding. Do you believe me?"

Charlotte was shaking. Weakly, she said, "I want to."

"Then just believe it. I won't betray you. I won't let you down. The first step is just waiting for us. I'm going to manage your father and your brother and sister. I'll get Henry behind me, I'll make sure he understands. We can't spend the rest of our lives apart. I can't let this go on. I'm doing this for all of us. You may not believe it, but I think that Charles and Carey feel how broken we are too. I see them slowly backing away, swimming away from us because the center is unstable. If we're not a family, then what is the point to any of it? Petunia needs her family. She needs a strong family, and it starts with you and me and your father."

They were quiet for a while. Charlotte was taking in what her mother had said and realized that she believed her. She was finally sharing her faults and owning up to them. That had never happened before.

"Mom." She stopped for a moment, consciously recognizing the reverence surrounding that word and how much she had missed saying it. "I wish things had been different. I wish we could all go back and change some of the things we said and did, including myself. I guess I wish that too." She was scared to death, making these concessions, making herself vulnerable.

"Honey. I'm sorry. I'm sorrier than I can say. I want us to start over. I want a relationship with you and Petunia. Can we try to make that happen?"

Charlotte remembered to breathe. "Maybe," she said softly.

Julia exhaled loudly. "Good. Maybe that's enough right now. Let me tell you about my plan. We are going to need your help. I told you I hired a private detective? His name is Alexander Macchi. He's an associate of Baach, McKenzie & Blake. Oliver told me I could trust him. He'll be in New York tomorrow and would like to meet you," Julia said, excited now.

"I don't understand. Why does he need to meet me? Did he find David? Is David coming too?" She panicked.

"Yes and no. Yes, he found David, but no, he won't let that bastard near you or Petunia."

David. Found. Holy shit.

"He wants to meet with me? You gave him my number?" She was uncertain.

"Yes, he has your number, and for that matter, he also knows where you live. I told him. But you can trust him, Charlotte. I promise you that. Over the time he's been working for me, he's been unquestionably respectful, honest, and gentlemanly. I know you can trust him, and he can help us. If you let him."

Trust was an awfully big word. Charlotte wasn't so sure about that, but she agreed to try.

Chapter 15

A lex Macchi called Charlotte the next day. She was hesitant but agreed to meet him that afternoon at her home. She felt she had nothing to lose by asking him to meet there since he already knew where she lived. James, thankfully, was available to babysit Petunia. The two of them were now at the park, and she looked at herself in the mirror, wondering if she was dressed okay to meet with a private detective. Not that she'd had any experience with that type of person.

She couldn't believe she was doing this. She nervously looked down at her soft-washed denim jeans and fitted white T-shirt and leaned into the mirror to see if she should wear the dangling jade, coral, and white earrings. How was she supposed to look for this meeting? She envisioned a cop in a polyester suit.

The doorbell rang, and she opened it to find an extremely handsome man on her stoop.

"Hello, Charlotte. I'm Alex Macchi," he said as he extended his hand.

She took it and said, "Hello. Please come in."

Alex followed her into the parlor level, a bold, confident, colorful room, yet filled with warmth and comfort. He looked around and said, "Thank you for agreeing to see me. I can only imagine how you must have felt when Julia shared the news that she'd hired me."

"Yes, as a matter of fact. She only just called me last night. It was a surprise. And not a pleasant one," she said, standing erect.

He turned, made his way to a chair, and gestured. "May I?"

Charlotte nodded and followed his lead. She perched on a chair opposite, waiting for him to respond.

He said carefully, "Did she discuss her reasons for hiring me?"

"Yes," she said, still guarded. "To find David."

"That's right. That's part of it, but she also shared several personal stories with me about your background with David and your relationship with the family," he said cautiously.

Mom was really branching out. Charlotte found it difficult to believe that she'd shared the truth about their fractured family relations and the horrors of Charlotte's love life with a stranger. This wasn't in her nature, or, for that matter, any of the Carrows.

She tilted her head questioningly. "Did she? Why don't you tell me what you've discovered about my family?" she said with an edge.

"Yes." He cleared his throat and clasped his hands. "I obviously know the factual details about the Carrows family and some history on your father's business successes.

I know of your home, Whispering Cliffs, and the charity work your mother and father participate in. But more importantly, Julia shared with me her personal relationship status with you. She told me about the relationship you had with the family prior to leaving to become a student in New York, the strained and distant relationship you had while in school, your relationship with Charles, Carey, and your father, your relationship with David, his theft of the Tsarina's Fancy from their home, and his abandonment of you."

She didn't let her composure slip, but her jaw unintentionally dropped. She closed it quickly.

"My mother told you everything about me? And about David?"

"Yes, she felt that for me to do the job properly, I would need to know why she was asking me to do it. She told me that it wasn't just about finding David, it was about mending the family relationships."

She stared at him and shook her head in disbelief. "If I believe her and you, my mother must be undergoing some type of metamorphosis. All of this behavior and sharing of personal family issues is not like her at all. For that matter, it's not like me at all. We don't usually share our private business and feelings with strangers."

"I respect that. I do, and I apologize if my presence in your life feels like an intrusion or lifting a veil on your privacy. I respect your privacy and the Carrows' privacy, and I can assure you that anything we share with each other will be kept confidential. However, I should mention that Julia is technically my client, and I would like to be as open as I possibly can with her. So, I'd want to tell her about our work but only the facts you're comfortable communicating. You have my word that I will not surprise you or sabotage you in any way. I really am here to help you. And to help Julia. And the Carrows family in any way I can."

Charlotte took a breath and looked away. She understood what he was saying, but it was difficult for her to open up. He appeared to be honest, and she was sure her mom had done a background check on him. But still. Charlotte had been wrong before.

She looked back at Alex and tried to take a measure of him. He was very handsome. He was beautifully dressed in an elegantly casual manner with dark-wash jeans and dark-blue shirt with a brown cashmere jacket. He was well groomed and had the polished manners of a gentleman. And there was something about his eyes.

"Alex. My mother told me you found David," she said, diving in.

"I did. I can share with you the long version or the short one. Which would be less painful?"

"I'm sure they will both be painful. But start by telling me where he is."

"São Paulo, Brazil," Alex said without emotion.

Brazil? What the hell was he doing in Brazil? He was hiding. That's what he was doing there. She felt herself grow red with anger thinking about him.

"I'm assuming you know that he is Petunia's father?" she said dryly.

"Yes. I know that. I am also assuming that he does not?" he said, an eyebrow raised.

"No. He doesn't. And I'd like to keep it that way. He means nothing to me. He is a loathsome human being, and he doesn't deserve to know." David had become a disgusting but fearful creature for her. She didn't like thinking about him in any way.

"I agree with you," he said with real compassion, his hands gently reaching out. "Let's take this one step at a time. Are you ready for me to tell you what I found out about him?"

She was ready. She needed to know. She gave a slight nod for him to begin.

"After David left you, he went to Dubai where he sold the Tsarina's Fancy to a man he met at the Metropolitan Museum. The man had traveled with the exhibition of the Romanov Jewels and was a supporter of the exhibition while it was in Dubai. David met him and remembered that he was very interested in the Tsarina's Fancy and had actually bid on it at auction against your father. The man agreed to purchase the ring from David and supply him with a new identity.

"David Torres," Alex continued, "is now known as David Cordoza. He had the fenced money wired to a bank in Rio de Janeiro, and he now lives in São Paulo. He works for several museums helping fundraise and support them. He is single, and as far as I could discover, has no other children."

My god. All the details coming together. Just like that. She knew where he was, what he did, and how he had pulled off the crime. Charlotte remembered that the exhibition of the Romanov Jewels took place while they were dating. When David found out that her real name was Charlotte Carrows, he must have put it all together from the day he'd moved in with her. She felt like she was on the verge of tears.

"Are you okay, Charlotte?" Alex said with concern, looking past her and noticing the glass doors leading outside. "Maybe we should go into the garden and get some air," he said as he stood and held out his hand.

She followed him, and they went outside. It was a good idea. The fresh air was welcoming.

"Just sit down here, and let's breathe for a moment," he said kindly.

"Thanks," she said tightly as she moved to sit at the table. "I'm okay."

"It's a lot to take in, Charlotte. You've been through what I am presuming is enormous pain. Can I get you something to drink? I'd be happy to retrieve something for you if you'd point me toward the kitchen?"

It was a kind gesture, and she said, "Yes. Thanks. The kitchen is upstairs, you'll obviously find it. I have an open bottle of Valpolicella on the counter. I'll have a glass of that. Pour one for yourself if you're interested. There are other options too."

"The Valpolicella sounds perfect. I'll be back in a minute." Alex went inside.

Damn you, David! Damn you, asshole. Damn you for using me! I will hate you forever. She held her head in her hands and tried not to cry. But she couldn't stop the tears. They came. Damn it! She got up and went inside for some tissues. She went back outside and stared at the sky and realized that David, or at least the memory of him, was now sitting directly beside her. She had to deal with it. But why? Why did she ever need to deal with him again? Her mother started this. She was getting angry at everyone now.

Alex returned with two glasses of wine. "Here we are. Thank you for sharing with me. Red wine is one of my passions." Looking at her, he noticed her defiant composure, so he changed the subject.

"Let me tell you a little something about myself. That would be fair, yes?" he said and smiled at her. He crossed his legs and leaned back to tell the story. "So, you know my name. I currently live in Los Angeles and work for Baach, McKenzie & Blake, but really, I'm only loosely affiliated with them. Julia contacted them, and they put her in touch with me. They use me for private inquiries. I graduated from law school at UCLA but never really felt the need to pass the bar. Or maybe I was just preoccupied with other interests. I'm originally from Brooklyn. A native New Yawka."

He noticed the way she perked up when he pronounced New York in his Brooklyn accent, so he smiled encouragingly and continued, "My family, my mother, my father, we're Italian. I have four brothers and one baby sister all still living in the area, except for me, of course. My father also owns a private investigation and security firm. One of my brothers works for him as well. I guess it runs in the blood."

She was listening, glad for the distraction, and picking up her glass for a sip, encouraged him to continue.

"After I graduated from Brooklyn College, I decided I wanted to see something more of the world than just New York. I guess I was considered a hipster, my nawse always in a book, everyone was always breaking my shoes." He gave a small smile at his joke and continued. "So, I decided I needed a change. I was accepted to law school at UCLA, and as I said, I graduated, but by that time I knew I wasn't interested in becoming a practicing attorney. My father had a few contacts on the West Coast, and one thing led to another, and I've now been working out there for the last eight years.

"Am I speaking too much?" he said, smiling at her with a lightness in his voice. "My accent, it comes and goes. It pops up more when I'm around my family, but I gotta watch that diction out in LA. I mean, fawget about it," he said, waving his hand through the air.

She was enjoying the story and realized Alex had a calming influence. She took another sip of her wine and said, "Do you see your family much since you live in LA?"

"Not as much as I'd like. I miss them a great deal. But my business in Los Angeles has been very successful, and it's difficult to walk away from that opportunity."

"So, you are close with them?" she said, curious.

"I'm very close with all of them. It's hard to keep track of everybody's busy lives, but I try to reach out to each of them as much as possible. It's hardest on my mom, my being gone. But she's happy that I'm happy. I'll probably try to see them this evening, unless of course, I'm needed here," he said, questioning.

"Needed here?" She pulled up. "No. I'm going to be fine. You can count on it."

He clapped his hands together softly and looked around. "It is such a beautiful day. I'm enjoying your garden. Where is Petunia?"

"She's with James, my tenant, at the park. Did you know that I have a tenant?"

"Yes. I know that. James has lived with you for almost a year?"

"Yes, I think we were lucky to find each other. He's been a good friend, and I trust him with Pinky."

"Pinky? That is something I didn't know. You call her Pinky?" he said and smiled.

Looking at him, Charlotte smiled for the first time. "Yes, sometime back I started calling her that name, and it just stuck. It's actually so like her, too."

She looked curiously at Alex who was smiling at her. "What else do you know about me, Alex?"

"I know that your father gifted this home to you before you attended NYU. I know you studied there and of course, that's where you met David Torres. Your mom told me that you graduated after Petunia was born. That's very admirable," he said. "I know a little about your tenant, James, and I know a little about where you work and where Petunia takes dancing lessons."

"You know she takes dance? How would you know that? Did my mom tell you?" she said, trying to piece it together.

He held her gaze and said calmly, "Because I was here in the city last month, and I followed you."

"You followed me? And Pinky? Why would you do that?" she said, slightly alarmed.

"I'm sorry to upset you, Charlotte. Let me explain," he said, putting his hands up gently before him. "My intention for following you was only to understand a little more about you and your circumstances. Your mother didn't really know how you were or how you were getting along. She did not ask me to spy on you, nor was that what I was really doing. It was a part of my job, this job, in particular, to help understand the situation from all the angles, about each of the individuals. Your mother presented a complicated picture. It's my experience that sometimes clients don't have an accurate picture, and before I proceeded I needed to see for myself what was happening here."

"What did you see then? What did you learn?" she asked defiantly, off-balance.

"I learned that you seem to be a very devoted mother to Petunia. I learned that you have supported her in every way possible and that you're very successful in your job at Frank and Son. It also appears as if you are not dating." He paused. "But I could be wrong about that?"

She was willing for him to know some of these things about her. It felt good to be called a devoted mother. But really, how much could he know about the rest?

"I find it difficult to trust them," she said cautiously, "and you would know why."

"I do. But that can change, Charlotte. You deserve to have a full life and to have a partner you can lean on. I hope that happens for you. Your happiness has become important to me," he said warmly.

He pulled up at his last comment. They looked at each other, each gauging the other's demeanor. He shook himself loose. "Perhaps I should be going. We've covered a lot of ground today, and I was really only hoping this initial introduction would help you understand the work that I do and a little about myself. Would you be willing to have dinner with me tomorrow night?"

She knew he was right. She was overwhelmed. She also realized that there was more to discuss, whether she wanted to or not.

"Tomorrow night works. Petunia doesn't have dance class, and I know James is available. How about we meet at Delmonico's at seven?"

"That sounds good. I'll make the reservations," he said and stood. He held out his hand to her. "Thank you for agreeing to meet with me. I look forward to seeing you again tomorrow. I'll show myself out."

She smiled at him as he left. Charlotte finished her wine in her garden as she thought about what to do.

———————————

After Alex left the previous evening, Charlotte had pieced together enough of the puzzle to grasp the situation. Her mother wanted David to be found, and she found him. Her mom wanted her dad to have an opportunity to confront David and satisfy himself with the knowledge that he was solely responsible for the theft. Although Charlotte hoped that by now even her father had realized that. What he would do with David once he had him alone was anyone's guess. Did she care? Should she care?

She cared enough that she was willing to meet with Alex again. She also found herself looking forward to spending time with him. Yesterday he was a stranger who came into her home and gave her information that was very difficult to hear. It definitely put her off-balance. Tonight, when she met with Alex again, she intended to be firmly in control of her emotions.

She chose a sleeveless, off-the-shoulder, asymmetrical, rose-pastel sheath dress. She was cinched with an appealing yet tasteful décolletage and wore her dark hair loose with a modest set of pearl earrings and necklace. She arrived promptly at seven o'clock.

Spying Alex at a nearby table, she told the maître d' that she was meeting with him. Walking alone to the table, she strode with confidence toward him, his wide smile encouraging. As she approached, both he and the waiter made a lunge to pull out her waiting chair. Alex won, and the waiter moved out of the way as he awkwardly grappled with the upset chair.

"Charlotte. Thank you for coming," he said, trying to recover his cool.

"You're welcome, Alex. It's good to see you again. I love your suit. You look very sharp," she said, noticing how the gray in his tie brought out the soft gray in his eyes, the way his dark hair fell a bit long onto his forehead.

"Thank you. You look very pretty this evening, too. That color is really lovely."

"It's such a hot evening. This felt cool to me." She gave him a pleasant smile.

"Would you like to order a cocktail or some wine?" he said as the waiter hovered nearby.

"Yes, some wine. Chardonnay would be refreshing."

"That sounds good. May I order something for us both?"

"Go ahead. Whatever looks good to you."

After ordering, he began to smooth the cloth on the table and rearrange the silver in front of him, composing himself before saying, "Charlotte. First of all, I want to let you know that I spoke with Julia last evening after we met. I told her, as I told you, that I would keep her informed of my movements since she is my client."

"You mentioned that. I didn't speak with her. What did you report to my mother?"

"I told her that we met at your home, and I brought you up to speed about David's activities and current where-abouts. I told her you handled it very well. I said we were going to be meeting again tonight for dinner and would begin to discuss our next steps. I hope that's all okay with you."

"Yes, that's fine. It's kind of a weird relationship though, don't you think, that a private investigator is calling my mother to tell her about me?" she said, her face flushing with some embarrassment.

"I know it's awkward, but remember, her goal is to reach a reconciliation with you. And not only for the two of you but for you and the entire family. I believe she has your best interests at heart."

"Well, she certainly has made you a believer. I think it will take me some time to trust the situation. But for the life of me, I can't come up with another explanation or ulterior motive. My god, listen to me. She is my mother. It's sad to think we've been reduced to this."

"Well, maybe that can be changed. Maybe you two can have a better relationship when this is all over. Would you like that, Charlotte?" he asked, sincerely curious.

It was an important question. She had to think about that. The little girl inside of her missed a family, and a mother and father. But she'd been so hurt by them. Accused and betrayed by them. Knowing that they had been hurting as well at least made her believe that some love remained and was reciprocal.

"Now that I have a daughter, my world view has changed so much," she said, staring at the table. "I can't imagine, I can't fathom a world where Petunia and I would be separated and estranged. It would break my heart."

"Julia told me she loves you very much. And Petunia too. On more than one occasion. I believe her. I think you should too," he said gently.

Charlotte considered this as they ordered their meal. What would that feel like if she just decided to take the leap and embrace as fact that her mother loved her and only wanted what was best for her? She realized that it would feel nice.

"Tell me," she said, changing the subject. "Did you say you actually saw David in person? I don't remember."

"Yes. I saw him. I went to São Paulo and a colleague of mine and I followed him for a couple of days. We did some checking up on him."

"How does he look?" she said carefully.

He considered. "He looked very relaxed and sophisticated. I don't know what he was like when you were with him, but he comes across as extremely confident. He's probably matured since the last time you've seen him. He has an excellent tailor."

This picture of him infuriated her. She didn't know what she expected or what she wanted from him, but she knew that anything he had created of himself was on her dime. Figuratively and literally.

"I guess robbing someone of a three and a half-million-dollar diamond will get you places!" she said with controlled bitterness.

"I believe what he did to you and your family, but especially to you, was terrible. He made a conscious decision to deceive you. He took calculated steps to achieve the successful swap of the stone. But he got lucky. And that, I believe, was fate, lending a hand for reasons we may never know."

Charlotte picked up her glass and realized it was empty. Alex promptly refilled it as she said, "It took me a very long time to get over the betrayal, Alex. When my parents accused me of participating in the theft, I was betrayed again. I can't tell you how much that hurt. The only reason any of this is okay is because he left me with a daughter."

"Yes, he did. Petunia is David's child as well," he said with some gravity.

She sat bolt upright. "I know he's her father, but he'll never be a part of her life. Never. Please understand that right now."

"I understand why you're saying this. And I agree with you. Believe me, I don't want, nor does Julia want, David anywhere close to either of you," he said, trying to calm her.

Charlotte relaxed a little, loosening the grip she had on her glass.

"But you're a smart woman. And more importantly, a wise and conscientious mother. Petunia will have questions about him. That day will come," he said, being honest.

She darkened thinking about it. "I know that. She has already asked questions about where her daddy is."

"And what did you say?" he said, studying her.

"I've been able to distract her from the issue for most of her life, but lately she's been asking a lot of questions about families in general. Specifically, why she only has me. We watched the movie *Heidi* with Shirley Temple the other day, and she got stuck on the grandfather. She wanted to know if she had one. And, of course, she actually has two living grandfathers, I believe, and grandmothers and an uncle and aunt, but how can I explain any of it to her without confusing her and upsetting her world? My brother has been out to see her, but that's it," she said with resignation, laying her fork aside, most of her food still untouched.

She'd never spoken with anyone about this subject before. She'd not realized until that moment that it would feel so comforting to do so.

"You might be able to distract her for a while longer, but once she's in school, she's going to notice she's different, and she is going to want to be able to have an answer for the other kids. Maybe during this process we can come up with an answer that will be helpful."

"I know you're right. I'm going to need something solid I can give to her to explain. But then, of course, I won't be able to change it later. More than anything in the world I don't want to hurt her," she said quietly.

"Then it's time we do something about the situation. David needs to be dealt with."

And there it was. She stared at Alex. It was nice that he used the word "we" and that he was willing to help them. But, how could he? She knew her mom's goal, or at least one of them, was to get David in front of her dad.

"I know Mom thinks the answer to all our problems is to get David to Dad and for him to do god knows what to him. But is it the answer? Won't it bring up just as many problems?" she said with real worry. "Specifically, problems for Petunia and me? Right now, she's safe from him because he doesn't know she exists, but once he does? What then? He could create all kinds of drama."

"I don't think he will, Charlotte," he said, shaking his head. "I think he's enjoying his life too much as a single man living a cosmopolitan life. I don't see him wanting to swap that role to be part-time dad. Even after he sees her for himself."

She was silent. They'd come to the crux of the problem. How would they get David back into the country and yet neutralize his relationship with Petunia?

"It's time that David be brought back to the States and make amends for hurting you so deeply," he continued. "It's time for him to pay for his crimes against the Carrows family. I have some ideas about how we could make that happen if you are ready to hear them."

She was.

They talked around the issue for a time and then Alex steered the conversation into safer areas. Over the course of their dinner, they got to know one another better, and it began to feel more like a date. They enjoyed each other's company.

"I was wondering," he said, "it's getting late, do you think we can continue this conversation again tomorrow? We have a lot to talk about, and if we get a fresh start, after a little less wine, we might be more productive," he said, smiling.

She smiled back, encouragingly. The dinner had started out on a challenging note but had turned into something very comfortable and even enjoyable. She realized she had been having a good time. She wasn't sure why she would be surprised by that. He was a wonderful, sensitive man who, as an added bonus, wasn't hard to look at.

"Pinky has dance tomorrow after work, and I don't want her around while we're discussing David. We'll need to meet on Wednesday. Why don't you pick the spot, and let me know?"

"That sounds great. Let's try something more casual? Can I pick you up at seven?"

"That works. Thank you for a really nice evening, Alex." She meant it. As they walked out of the restaurant, Alex's hand gently pressed against her back as he held the door open for her. Their eyes locked. There was an intensity there, and for a fleeting moment, she thought that he might kiss her. She was highly disappointed when it didn't happen.

———————

Wednesday dawned, and Charlotte woke up excited. She knew why. Alex was going to pick her up this evening, and they would be spending more time together. What was it about him that was making her excited? She couldn't deny there was a physical attraction, and that didn't feel bad at all. But it was more than that. She really enjoyed his company. He made her so comfortable. And she was actually startled when she realized that one of the reasons she felt that way was because she could be honest with him.

It was easy to be around him because he knew who she really was. He knew more about her than anyone else in her life. There was no effort to remember herself and not give anything away. To hide who she was and where she lived. To hide her past with David and the theft and her broken family. She didn't need to worry about any of that because he already knew. It was a tremendous relief, and until just then, she didn't realize the weight she had been carrying.

She also decided, after she had time to think, that she was going to accept his opinion that her mother loved her and wanted what was best. That gave Charlotte two options. Accept it, reciprocate, and try to rebuild a relationship, or two, accept that her mother wanted to mend their relationship, but she would not.

As frightened as she was of getting hurt again, she believed, and maybe always knew, that she was a creature of the light side of life. Her nature would always want her to love.

Alex told her their evening would be more casual, and she didn't know quite what that meant, but she assumed dinner would be involved. After work, she changed into black leggings with a white tank covered by a loose, sleeveless, white cotton vest, which was loosely belted and hung to just above her knees. She finished the look with black sneakers and simple hoop earrings.

Alex arrived at seven o'clock, and they took a cab to a bar in Chelsea.

"One of my brothers is a cop in the tenth precinct, and I meet him here from time to time. They have a pretty decent burger," he said as they were seated.

Charlotte looked around, and although she had never been in the bar before, she immediately felt safe and at home as Alex greeted a couple of the staff.

After they ordered some iced tea and burgers, Alex dove directly into the work at hand. "When I left you on Monday I got the impression that you were ready to discuss the next steps regarding David, is that correct?"

"I am. I realize that I'm going to need to either face him directly or, at least, face the situation for Petunia's sake. But my mom feels really strongly that we get him to Dad. I just don't have any idea how to do that, and I can't think of what it will mean for Pinky and me," she said, confused.

"I know it's a lot to think about, but I have a few ideas I'd like to run past you. The first thing we need to agree upon is that the plan would accomplish exactly what Julia is expecting, bringing David to Henry. I agree with her that this will go a long way toward helping restore the relationships in the family. I also think you and Petunia deserve to have a family again," he said, raising his eyebrows, not in a question, but as stating a fact. He took a big bite of his burger.

"Well, my family can be very difficult, but they're all I have. I think it would help Pinky, though, to know it's not just the two of us in this world, and that there are others who care about her," she said, taking a bite of her burger as well.

"Okay then. I have some ideas, but I'm not sure how you're going to like them. They'll require a big leap from you. You're going to need to come out of the closet, Charlotte. You're going to need to let the world in on your secret life as a Carrows."

That stopped her. "What are you saying? You mean I have to tell everyone that I am related to the Carrows family?"

"That is exactly what I'm saying. We need to get David's attention. We need him to reach out to you. The bait would be twofold: your public revelation that you are a Carrows and the interest that would create, and two, that he has a daughter."

This was too much. "And bring the devil directly back into our lives? Into Petunia's life? Why would I do that? The consequences are enormous. The risk? God, to see him again? I don't want to do that!"

He said compassionately, "This is the path that we're going down. If David is to be brought back to the States to face the consequences of his actions, then you will need to see him, and a resolution must be reached in regards to your daughter."

"What kind of resolution?" she said in panic. "Why would I need to give him anything? I don't know how I feel about any of this. I know Petunia needs to know *something* about her father, but I know I don't want him in our lives."

"That's a start. We can work with that. And as I said, I don't honestly believe he would want to be a part of your lives. But I can't be sure. I *believe*, Charlotte, that he will be willing to negotiate. And I believe Henry Carrows will do an excellent job of that when the time comes."

"So, what is this plan? What are you proposing? That we make Petunia the bait?" she said defensively.

"I know that sounds harsh and feels wrong, but she won't have to know about it."

At her expression of outrage, he hurried forward. "Let me tell you my idea. It isn't a fait accompli, and we won't be doing anything you're not comfortable with. So please remember that you're in control here. But my plan is that we plant an article or two in the *New York Daily News* and the *New York Post* about you along with a picture of you and Petunia. Her age would be prominently listed," he said, knowing she would understand the implications of that.

She blanched. Sick with the unimaginable image of Petunia not only in the paper but in front of David's face.

"I thought that you could attend the upcoming Tribeca Ball," Alex continued. "I would be sure to have your picture published. I have some connections who would do that. The picture of you would have your real name, Charlotte Carrows. We'd plant another article the following day with a picture of you and Petunia together. She wouldn't even have to know she was being photographed. I could manage that. And, again, I could guarantee placement in at least one, if not several, publications. David will see the articles and put two and two together. He will realize that Petunia is his daughter. We will have his attention." He sat back, waiting for her response.

She was startled but smart enough to realize that it might actually work. After a restrained moment to collect herself, she said, "You realize that you're asking me to change my life. To change her life. To put ourselves at risk for drama, scrutiny, and media attention. Something I have worked my entire life to avoid. I don't know if I can do that."

It was a crazy plan. What was she doing? This was all going so fast. She went on. "And if we do get David's attention and he does realize that he has a daughter, what then? What will happen next? What will he do? What will I do? How will you get him to Los Angeles?" she said, her confusion and panic building.

He sat back and said, "I don't get him to Los Angeles. You do."

"What do you mean? What can I do?" she said, her eyes wide with shock.

"You would lure him. You would con him. You would convince him. You would fly to São Paolo and bring him back to Los Angeles with you," he said, calmly laying it out.

Too much. Too much was happening here. She needed time to think. She saw where this was going, and she couldn't stomach it. She was done.

"Alex, I understand what you're proposing. But I need some time to think about this. I need to leave," she said as she began to gather her things.

"Please, Charlotte," he said, reaching out his hand, trying to calm her. "I understand, and I agree it's very important for you to take time to consider this. But before you leave, I want you to remember two things," he said and paused.

"Well, what? I'm listening," she said, her bag in hand, one foot in the aisle, ready to slide out of the booth.

"If you do this, you will have some peace with your family, and I believe you will find peace with yourself. You will also have a resolution about what to do with the David issue, and you will deal with the fact that he is Petunia's father. And lastly, the Tribeca Ball is next week."

She left.

Riding in the taxi on the way home, Charlotte tried to process what Alex had said. He wanted her to change her entire life. To come out of the closet as a Carrows. To con David. To speak with David. To f-ing see David! She hated him! She never wanted to see him again. Why would she do all of this? *Petunia and I are doing fine!* There was a possibility David would never even return to the United States. If she did nothing, he might never even find out he had a daughter! *Things could continue on as they have been*, she told herself.

Over the course of the long evening getting ready for bed she continued to worry. There were pressing problems. Her mother wanted to rebuild their relationship. Charlotte didn't think she could turn her back on that desire. Petunia needed protection from David if he ever did discover her existence. She also deserved answers to her questions. Petunia also had the right to know she had more family. She would find out eventually, somehow, and then it might be too late, and she might resent Charlotte for keeping so many secrets from her. Was it possible that one day Petunia would turn away from her as she had done to her own mom? For all she knew, Carey would show up on their doorstep any day now and just blurt out the entire family history. What would Petunia think of her then?

She had also become aware over the last few days that she enjoyed not carrying the weight of all her secrets. She felt normal, freer, and lighter. Maybe it was time to stop worrying so much about other people's reactions to her background and focus on just living her life as herself. Maybe, in the long run, she would have more friends because she could be more honest and not hold herself back. She *had* been holding herself back, too. From every-one. It wasn't joyous. It wasn't the way she knew she should live.

This was her life, and by hiding from everyone, she had been cheating herself of the opportunity to make deep and lasting relationships. Her family started her on this path, and David and his actions had furthered it. This meant that she had been living her life as a reaction to others rather than for her true self. Alex had helped her see that.

She realized that she really had no choice at all. She would agree to the plan.

Chapter 16

The Tribeca Ball was founded in 1982 by Andy Warhol to celebrate the human art form. The New York Academy of Art was the beneficiary of the event, which has supported hundreds of emerging and new artists. It was also a formal, star-studded evening attended by the glittering New York society crowd, celebrities, and even former presidents.

Alex told Charlotte he was relieved when she agreed to his plan. He said he felt a huge responsibility now that the events and details were in place, and he knew this would alter her world forever. He said he did not take that lightly. Charlotte appreciated his understanding and his comradery.

Julia had overwhelmingly approved of the plan too as it also meant that Charlotte would formally take her place in society as a Carrows. She knew Henry would be delighted with this news. Julia had secured two tickets to the ball, and since the event was also sponsored by Van Cleef & Arpels, she contacted the jeweler to arrange for Charlotte to have on loan any of their treasures that her ensemble would require. She had also given Charlotte unlimited access to her charge cards to go shopping.

That was the only part Charlotte enjoyed. She purchased an alluring floor-length, backless black velvet halter dress with a deep V plunging neckline and a small train that pooled beautifully. The massive diamond drops on loan from Van Cleef were stunning.

Petunia was excited the evening of the event as her mom rarely dressed in such super fancy clothes, and the jeweler had sent a security escort to accompany them. At six o'clock, the doorbell rang, announcing Alex's arrival. Petunia ran to the door to open it.

Alex stood on the step wearing a handsome black Tom Ford tuxedo. "Good evening! Is your mother, Charlotte, home?" he said formally to Petunia.

"Hi!" She waved at him. "Are you Alex? Mom said it was okay to let you in," she said as she theatrically bowed before letting him enter.

"You should see Mom!" Petunia continued with great enthusiasm. "That's a *guard*. He's guarding her diamonds!" She whispered the last and pointed to a nicely dressed gentleman.

Alex smiled at her and introduced himself to the security representative and James, who would be staying with Petunia while they were gone.

Shaking his hand, Alex said, "Hello, James, I've heard so much about you. All good. Thank you for everything you do for Charlotte and Petunia. I'm glad she has such a good friend."

Charlotte had taken time the evening before to have a private conversation with James. She didn't want him to be blindsided by the news that would be released in the press about her real name. James, to his credit, did not blink. He just gave her a hug and said that no matter what her name, they would always be friends. Charlotte actually cried. With joy. It felt really wonderful to be loved for who she was.

Alex looked up the stairs as Charlotte walked down. "Wow! You take my breath away," he said with his hand over his heart, smiling up at her.

"Alex, you look amazing! So handsome! Did you meet everyone?" She beamed.

"Pinky, how do we look?" she asked.

"You're so pretty, Mama! Can I take your picture now?" she said, dancing.

"Alex, would you mind? I said she could take a picture of us before we left," Charlotte said as she positioned herself next to him.

"Good idea. Let's take some with James and Petunia too," he said, grinning at Petunia, watching her light up.

Charlotte didn't think the evening could get any better than this, but she was wrong.

The Tribeca Ball had a step and repeat for the arriving guests to have their pictures taken by the press. Alex and Charlotte had agreed that this exercise would be for her alone. She gave her name as Charlotte Carrows and posed for the cameras. Alex needed to remain anonymous, at least for the time being.

The ball had cocktails from 6:00 to 8:30, after which the dinner and dancing began. Over cocktails, Alex and Charlotte toured some of the six floors of art, which had studios filled with artists and models at work. The evening didn't disappoint them with all of the lively entertainment, and it went by very quickly. But the most important moment came at the end of the evening on the stoop of her building.

Standing on the top step, Charlotte had her key in her hand, nervous, highly aware of Alex's presence next to her and the awkward goodnight they were facing at her front door. She realized it wasn't a real date, but at that moment it felt like nothing more. She turned her face to look at Alex, uncertain about how to end the evening when he leaned over and lightly kissed her. It couldn't have felt more perfect.

The next day, Julia excitedly called Charlotte to get the details about the ball. She was overjoyed looking at a picture of her beautiful daughter in the *New York Post* when she called. It was all coming together, and she and Charlotte were speaking. So far so good.

Earlier that week, Alex had taken a picture of Charlotte and Petunia on the street. He and Charlotte had prearranged a moment for them to stop where he would be positioned across the street from them. Pinky didn't see him take the picture. It was published two days after the Tribeca Ball in the *Post* and the *West Villager* newspapers. Julia also forwarded both pictures to the *Palisadian-Post* and *LA Times*. They were only too happy to publish them.

Chapter 17

David Torres Cordoza was in the habit of reading many newspapers daily. He needed to be kept current about what was happening in the city, as well as the world, to retain his relevance and his clients' interests. He used to subscribe to the New York papers and the *Los Angeles Times*, but he eventually gave up the printed publications and just viewed them online. It was a part of his day to day that he never abandoned.

When he saw the picture of Charlotte in the *New York Post*, he was shocked. It had been so quiet on that front. Not a word or whisper about her, ever. It was like she didn't exist. He hadn't been able to follow her life due to that fact, but he never stopped wondering what she was up to. And suddenly, there she was. At the Tribeca Ball, in an evening gown, proclaiming herself not as Charlotte McGee but as Charlotte Carrows for god's sake! His mouth hung open. His pulse rapidly picked up as he scanned the picture and the article. God, she was beautiful. He always knew she was, but she had grown into a magnificently alluring woman.

And those jewels didn't hurt either. Wow! After all this time, he hadn't expected to ever see her again. He'd kept up with the Carrows family through the California papers, but oddly, there was never anything on Charlotte.

Two days later, he was even more surprised when there was another picture of Charlotte in the *New York Post* but this time with a little girl. The caption read: *"Charlotte Carrows with her daughter, Petunia."*

What was he looking at here? Charlotte had a daughter? He stared at the picture. How old was she? Maybe three or four? The blood drained from his face. "Wait a minute. Hoooollllllyyy Shit. Holy Shit. She has a daughter? My daughter?" He started screaming, "What the fuck?" He did the math. "It's got to be mine. What the fuck did she name her? Petunia? Really, Charlotte?" He stared at the picture of the young girl. Was he a father? She must have been pregnant when he left. Why didn't she tell him? Maybe she didn't know?

But the math was right, and Petunia wasn't adopted. She looked exactly like Charlotte only with a more olive complexion, like him. Charlotte wouldn't have screwed around on him. No way. She fucking worshiped him. And after he took off, she wouldn't have just jumped in the sack with anyone. She wouldn't do that. "She has to be mine. Shit. Unbelievable." He had a daughter?

Over the course of the next few days, David spent most of his time scouring the internet looking for more pictures or birth records or anything on them. But he couldn't find a thing. Probably because she usually went by stupid and silent Charlotte McGee and not Charlotte Carrows. He was fascinated by this turn of events.

David had become, once again, discontent. His time in São Paulo was absorbing and exciting and initially had been filled with the liberation of worrying about money. But he hadn't spent his $1,750,000 judiciously. Eventually, he realized he had to start making his own money again rather than just enjoying it.

He began to daydream of easier times. His life was surrounded by the wealthy and the very wealthy, and he realized that the money and comfort he had was not enough. He wanted more. He had always been envious of the rich, but it had now turned into a quiet seething and resentment that he had to work for a living and most of them did not. His years in São Paolo had also given him an appreciation for his life in the United States, and as often happens with expats, he was homesick.

His parents were another concern. Over the last four years, David had seen them twice. He found the travel to Mexico to be grudgingly expensive. He resented the time he had to take out of his schedule to visit them. He could have flown them into São Paulo, but that would just raise questions from them. As it was, David helped support them, so they didn't ask too many questions about his life. The overriding theme recently, however, was the ten-year expiration of their time bar, which would allow the process of immigration to the United States to begin. But David would have to live in the United States for that to happen. Their dream of reuniting with David and their close friends and family in California was near if only David would begin the process. But first, he needed to move back to the US.

The pressure was building. He began to plan. He still had some money and an apartment in São Paulo that could be sold for a nice profit, but it was nowhere near the initial $1,750,000 he had had in his hands when he left Dubai. He could afford quite a lot for a person of average means in a big city, but he didn't consider himself, nor would he ever want to be considered, average. If he were to return to the United States, he would need to decide where to live. The dream would be returning to New York City as a big hit. He had some money, his wardrobe, his education, his resume, his references, and his experience to take with him. On paper, he was a big deal in São Paulo, but would that translate to New York City? That was a different world to conquer. He wasn't afraid exactly, he just considered the problems and knew there would be challenges. Where else would he want to live? San Francisco came to mind and possibly Los Angeles. But he didn't know if it would be safe to live in California and be so near the Carrows family. Part of the job requirement in David's world was to socialize and build a network of mutually beneficial relationships that he could parlay into cash commissions. Accomplishing this in California might mean running into the Carrows.

Had they ever found out the ring was stolen? If they had, he didn't think they reported it, but how would he know for sure? Did they have any leads on what happened? Could they tie it back to him? If they discovered it only recently, they might never even think of him. After all, he had been out of Charlotte's life for years.

All of these thoughts had been in his mind over the last year, and then, suddenly, fate stepped in and handed him something else. He had a daughter. A Carrows daughter. And he hadn't been told. Didn't fathers have rights? Shouldn't he have been told? But how could she have told him? He'd lied to her and disappeared. How would she have found him?

More importantly, how could he use this new twist to his advantage? It looked as if Charlotte had finally come out of the closet as a Carrows. About time too, idiot. If she was officially a Carrows, and there had been a family reunion of sorts, that might mean she was back in their good graces and had access to their money. What if he could win her back and become the husband of Charlotte Carrows? He would have access to her home and privileges and finances. He could set himself up again in the US, and he would finally be able to bring his parents back from their fucking perdition in Mexico.

He walked over to a nearby shelf and picked up an engraved gold box. He opened it, surprised it still worked. The light came on, illuminating the gold bar nestled in silk. He picked up the bar and thought back to that night, that wonderful night when his life had dramatically changed. The silly gold bar had been a fake, something he got around to checking on once he had settled in the city.

"What a joke," he scoffed, thinking about it now. "You may have given me a piece of crap, but I gave you a granddaughter. I guess that makes us related now, Henry," he said, amused.

It might be time to give Charlotte a call. He bought a burner phone and thought about what to say to test the waters.

Chapter 18

Charlotte and Alex were waiting. This was the strategy. If David reached out to *her,* then he wouldn't be suspicious. It couldn't be the other way around. Plan B was not in the works, not just yet. In the meantime, Charlotte began spending all of her free time with Alex. It was delightful.

After her "coming out" ball, as she started referring to it, her life began to change. First came the conversations she had to have with the people in her life who didn't know about her true circumstances and identity. Her boss, Jon, was the first one she needed to deal with.

"Hello, Charlotte," Jon said cautiously when she came in for work. His feet on the desk, the newspaper in his hands, he said, "I didn't know if I would see you again. Imagine my surprise this morning when I opened the paper and found out that you are actually Charlotte *Carrows,* related to the Carrows family in California? It reminded me of people who win the lottery and then immediately quit their jobs. I'm surprised to see you," he said with a sharp tone.

"Jon, I know I have a lot of explaining to do, and I owe you an explanation. I consider you a friend, not just a colleague," she said, moving toward him.

"Do you keep all your friends in the dark about your true identity?" he said, putting the paper down.

"As a matter of fact, I do. Or I have. No one knew that I was related to the Carrows family. My real name *is* Charlotte McGee, legally, but my parents are Henry and Julia Carrows. I changed my name when I turned eighteen. It's a long story."

He stared at this new person in front of him. He didn't know what to make of all this. It was still Charlotte, yet it wasn't. His trust in her was being challenged, but looking back, from her first day with him, he recalled that she was always selling herself as someone the job required her to be. He'd watched her transform herself many times to become the person that was needed to close a deal. Maybe she hadn't lied to him as much as he initially thought.

"So, you are Charlotte Carrows. McGee. I don't understand any of this," he said, shaking his head.

"I know. I'm really sorry for lying to you. I should have told you the truth, but it wasn't something I was sharing with anyone."

She took a seat across from him.

"Only one other person in New York City knew who I really was, and when I told him the truth, he nearly destroyed me by using me. Since then, I've found it incredibly difficult to trust people." She paused, kneading her hands.

"But the thing is, recently, things have changed, and I discovered that keeping my identity hidden wasn't making me happy or keeping me safe. In fact, it was doing just the opposite. It was making me unhappy by my constantly having to keep silent and lie and pretend. It was making my relationships inauthentic, and I couldn't do it any longer. To myself mostly and to my friends, to you, but also to my daughter. I needed to shed the secrets of my life while she was still young. I came to the realization that Petunia deserves to know who she is.

"I'm really sorry if I hurt you, Jon. There're a lot of people I'm going to need to talk to. Being a Carrows in public is going to change my life in so many ways. It was easier to be Charlotte McGee, or at least, I thought it was.

"Can you forgive me for lying to you?" she said, sincerely concerned.

He began to understand after listening to her that she was right, her world would change. Maybe he should try to be more understanding. He couldn't know what it felt like to be in her shoes. But he knew money changed people. She was right about that. From now on, people would treat her differently.

"Charlotte, since the day you walked into my life you have been an enigma. I never really understood who you were. I liked you, I still like you. I value our friendship as well. You're right, this will change your life, but I don't want to be one of those people who sees you differently now. I'd like to remain your friend and colleague if you're still up for that?"

"Jon, yes, of course, you're my friend. Thank you for understanding and for saying that." She put her hand on her heart. "I feel so relieved."

"What about your job here?" he questioned. "Are you still going to work for me?"

"I suppose some people will wonder what I'm doing leasing office space. But, hey, we both know I'm good at it," she said as she laughed a little.

"That you are!" he said and smiled. "If you quit, it will be a huge loss for me."

She shook her head. "I just don't know what I'm going to do. I really love working here, but can you give me a little time? There're some things happening right now that are really confusing. Some things that pushed me out of the closet, so to speak. I'm going to need some time off to figure it out."

Jon paused, then got up and walked over to her. She stood up as he wrapped her in a big hug. "Charlotte McGee Carrows, I would do anything for you. And someday soon, I'm going to need to hear the long version of why you're working here with me, but in the meantime, I'm here to help if I can. Just let me know what I can do."

———————

Alex was spending as much time with Charlotte as she would allow. Since he had already been introduced to Petunia, he was welcome in their home, and he found himself spending several evenings with the two of them. Her child was adorable. The freckles across her nose were more prominent than those on Charlotte's; he thought she was very special.

It was comfortable and easy and extremely exciting. Alex and Charlotte got to know each other better, and it was obvious, yet unspoken, to both of them that their relationship was no longer just about business. It was going in a different direction. He knew that he loved her the moment he saw her on her stairway the night of the Tribeca Ball. His confliction over being a professional and keeping their relationship casual was impossible when he was around her. And that was the only place he wanted to be.

Petunia was in bed, and they were in her kitchen, standing at the sink, cleaning up after their dinner. Charlotte was washing a few of the dishes that didn't fit in the dishwasher, and Alex was drying. "Have you been spending time with your family?" she asked. "Are you still staying at your brother's house?"

"Yeah, Tony, in Brooklyn. He's married. The cop I told you about? They don't have any children yet, but I think they're trying. They've got a spare room, so basically, I'm sleeping in the nursery, or their nursery-to-be," he said, amused.

"That sounds nice." She smiled at him. "Are you surrounded by baby stuff and sleeping under a mobile?" She laughed.

"Not quite. Not yet. I've also been visiting the rest of the family when I can too. My mom and dad are pretty happy having me around. We all miss each other, I think."

"I can't imagine what it would be like to have a big happy family with everyone getting along and loving each other. I don't have to tell you mine was very different," she said, trying to push a stray lock of hair off of her face with the back of her hand.

"For the most part, it's wonderful. It hasn't been perfect, but I realize I'm very lucky," he said, helping her tuck the hair behind her ear.

"Have you thought about moving back to New York?" she said, focused again on the dishes.

"I think about it. They have a different lifestyle here than the one I enjoy on the West Coast. Every time I come back for Christmas, I'm reminded why I love LA."

Their hands touched as she handed him a pan. The tension between them was palpable. "Alex, you haven't said if you're dating anyone. I don't know why I was assuming no. Are you seeing someone back in California?"

He warmed to the topic. "I was seeing someone, on and off, a few years ago, and I date, but my work keeps me busy. I guess I haven't found the right person. How about you?" he asked, assuming she would have mentioned it by now but not completely sure.

"There hasn't been anyone for me, not really, not since Petunia was born. I went out on a couple of dates, but there was never a spark that made me want to continue. I guess if I were honest, there was always my identity problem that I knew I would have to deal with if I wanted to have a true relationship with someone. It just seemed like there were too many obstacles to overcome. It's been difficult for me to trust men since David."

He considered this beautiful woman and the sadness she had experienced not only because of David but because of the self-imposed box that she had put herself in. He understood it, partly. But there was still a lot he did not know.

She wiped her hands on a towel, the dishes complete, and walked past him. He reached out, stopping her, and turned her toward him. He couldn't help himself. He had to know if she wanted him as much as he did her. His hands on her shoulders, he slid them down her arms until they reached her hands. Holding them, he looked into her beautiful green eyes and said, "Well, Charlotte, since those obstacles aren't here now and not in *our* way, I'm wondering if you might want to explore a relationship with me?" He was encouraged by a look only a woman interested would give him.

Emboldened, he continued softly, searching her eyes, exploring their depths. "God knows I felt something spark when we kissed. How about you?"

"Mm hmmm," she murmured softly.

They looked deeply into one another's eyes, taking off the veils and revealing their full intent. He looked down at the hands he was holding, turning the palms over and examining them. He brought one up and kissed it tenderly.

"I think you're wonderful, Charlotte. I adore you. From the first moment I laid my eyes on you, I swear to god, my heart beat faster. Every time I'm near you, I'm torn up, working hard to stop myself from pulling you into my arms. It's not technically ethical, you see, but I can't help myself."

"Well, are your ethics breakable, Mr. Macchi?" she said lightly, smiling.

"I'd break them in a second for you," he said in a hoarse voice, his breath caught for a moment.

"Okay then, Alex," she said seductively, "I think it's time for you to stop treating me like a client and start treating me like any other woman you'd like to date."

He didn't wait to be asked twice. He grabbed her, and they kissed. For the first time deeply. What happened next was, without question, well worth the wait for both of them.

Chapter 19

It took about a week. David called.

Alex wasn't around. It was late at night, but Charlotte knew it was him as soon as the phone rang. She felt sick. She and Alex had prepared for this. She knew what she needed to sell. First step, appear angry. No problem with first step.

"Hello?"

"Charlotte, it's me," he said simply.

My god. It was him. She gave him silence.

"Charlotte, are you there?"

"I'm here, David. What do you want?"

"I'm calling to say hello. I thought we should talk."

"Talk about what? What do you want?"

"I think you know why I'm calling."

"No, I don't. Why would I speak to you?"

"Okay, I'll tell you why. I think you owe me an explanation to start with."

"An explanation for what, David? What are you talking about?"

"I saw the picture in the *Post.* I saw the picture of you in the *Post* with our daughter."

Silence.

"Your daughter?"

"You know she's mine. I know it, and you know it. There's no need to pretend or draw this out. I knew you well enough to know that you didn't sleep around. And I'm no idiot, the math is right. Petunia? Is that her name? Petunia McGee Carrows? My daughter."

Silence.

"What about it, David? What do you care? You didn't care about me or our relationship. Why would you care about her?"

"Don't you think I deserved to know about her? As it happens, I do care, very fucking much, that I have a daughter."

"What did you want me to do, David, telephone you on Mars? You left me! You abandoned me, asshole!"

"You're right, I know about that part, and I'm sorry about all that, I really am. But you could have found me through my parents, you knew where they were. You could have found us."

"Like I'd want to reach out and find you? Why in the world would I want you in my life? In your daughter's life? You don't deserve either of us."

"Well, that might be true. Maybe. But I deserved to know. If I had found out, if I had known you were pregnant when I left, I might not have! I might have stayed. I know I was confused, and the pressure on me was more than I could handle, but I knew you wouldn't have understood what I was going through. I have my pride too, so I just left. Call me a coward, call me an asshole. Fine. But at least I didn't give birth to someone's child and then hide it from them."

"Hide her from you? You are incredible. Don't try to turn this around on me. You're the one who left. You're the one who *never* looked back. I'm still here. You knew where to find me. Asshole."

Silence.

"Okay, you're right. I know you're right. I was wrong. I shouldn't have done that to you. I'm sorry. I really am. But, Charlotte, I have rights. She's my daughter too."

BOOM!

"Fuck you, David," she said and hung up.

Perfect. Not one word about the stone. David hadn't known what to expect from Charlotte when he called, but he figured he had nothing to lose and maybe something to gain. She was really angry with him, that was obvious, but he wasn't worried about that. He *had* been worried that the Carrows had tied him to the theft of the ring. But surely, she would have mentioned that? It was kind of a big deal, and it would have been her ace to keep him away. But she didn't use it, which had to mean they didn't know.

Maybe they were stupid? He could use stupid. He gave it another day and then called again. *Let's ramp it up.*

São Paulo was three hours ahead of New York. He waited until he thought she would be the most vulnerable and alone but still awake. He didn't want her to sleep.

She answered the phone at 11:00 p.m.

"Hi, Charlotte, it's me again."

Dead air.

"Listen, I know you're mad at me. I know what I did was wrong. But can we please just talk? Will you talk to me?"

"What do you want, David? No, I don't want to talk to you. We don't have anything to talk about. You need to stop calling me."

"Please just listen to me, okay? I've got to talk to you. I can't get you and Petunia out of my mind. I keep staring at her picture. She is so beautiful, Charlotte. She actually looks like both of us, don't you think? All your beauty and a little of mine? Can we talk about her? What is she like? Has she ever asked about me?"

"No, she hasn't asked about you. She doesn't know you exist. And she never will," she said coldly.

"But I do exist. We both know that. I could have been a father to her. I still can be. Don't you think she deserves to have a father? Don't you think she needs to know who I am and that I care? If you had given me the chance, she might have had me all along. But you took that from me."

"Are you nuts? You took her out of your own life by leaving me! You left me! You didn't look back!"

"I know I did all that, and I tried to explain why I did it, but it was complicated. I'm sorry, I really am, but I can't undo it now. We have to look at where we are right now, today, and where we go from here."

"We don't go anywhere. You are no one to us."

He sat quietly for a while, listening to her breathe.

Very calmly, he said, "You know that's not true. I am Petunia's father. I only just found out about her. I did not abandon her. I didn't know."

"David, I am going to hang up now. You are never to call me again. Do you understand? Never call me again. We have nothing more to say to each other."

She hung up.

———————————

He called again the next evening. "Thank you for picking up, Charlotte. Before you hang up, I need to tell you something. I've decided that I need to see Petunia and that I need to be a part of her life. My parents and I discussed the situation, and as you know, they will hopefully be moving back to the US in the near future. When I told them they had a granddaughter, they were over the moon. It's a dream come true for them. My mother cried. But then I told her the circumstances and that her granddaughter is nearly four years old and that she was secretly kept from me and from them, for that matter. And she wept again.

"This is all very emotional for us," he continued. "I showed them Petunia's picture from the paper. My daughter. Their granddaughter. They had a lot of questions, but they remembered you from when we were dating. I know you never met them, but I told them about you. They have no other children as you'll recall. I was the only child my mother carried to term. They want to be a part of their granddaughter's life, and I want that too. We are going to have to come to some terms, Charlotte. You know that, don't you?"

He didn't get a response, but he heard her crying. Perfect.

"David," she said. "Please don't do this. Please just go away. Don't make this complicated for her. If you really cared about her, you wouldn't do anything to upset her world. You wouldn't do anything to hurt her. She wouldn't understand. Just leave us alone."

"I don't think I can do that. Not now. Not anymore. Not now that I know she's out there. I think she will understand. She's smart, right? How do you think she is going to feel when she finds out that you kept her from me? From her family? You're the one who's hurt her."

"You're twisting this, you ass. I won't let you come within breathing distance of her. I will fight you with everything I have. My resources are deep, David. You don't stand a chance."

"I think you're wrong about that. And I think you already know you're wrong. All I have to prove is DNA. Fathers have rights. Once the court system finds out that you kept her from me, that I didn't abandon her, but on the contrary, only just found her, they will see it my way. I will win."

"What do you want? Do you want money? Do you want blackmail money? You'd stoop so low as to blackmail us, you crazy bastard?"

"I don't want money. I want to see my daughter. I want to build a relationship with her."

"You can't win. You may think you can, but once a judge finds out you left me and never called again, they will side with me. I will make your life miserable. You'll never get her."

"That's not where we should be going with this. You're being unreasonable. And if you want to play games with me and threaten me with all the Carrows legal maneuvering strategies, I have a strategy too. I also have a powerful friend. One you don't like. The press."

She hung up.

———————————

He called again. It was becoming his routine. Charlotte and Alex were very encouraged that he was falling into their trap, believing she was emotionally vulnerable to him.

"Hello, David."

"Have you calmed down? Can we talk? Please, we need to talk. Can we just work something out here? I don't want to threaten you, but you threatened me. All I want is to spend some time with Petunia and for her to know that she has a father. Please work with me on this, Charlotte. We can work something out, I'm sure of it."

She took a deep breath. "Okay, David, let's meet and discuss it. I agree we need to talk."

"I'm so glad that you feel that way. It's such a relief to hear you come around."

"I'm not coming around, let's just meet and talk. Where are you?"

"My work has me traveling quite a bit. For now, I'm living in Rio."

"Brazil? You're in Brazil?"

"Yes. It's a temporary assignment. I've moved around a lot since I last saw you. Brazil is a wonderful country. I'd been considering making it my home, but my parents need me in the States, and now, of course, there is Petunia to consider. I'll be making arrangements soon to relocate. In fact, I've already started."

"When do you think you'll be moving back?"

"I'm not sure. In a few months? Maybe six? There are a lot of details involved."

"I don't think this can wait six months. Can I come and see you now?"

"Come to Rio? Well, yes. That would work. I'm glad you're as anxious as I am to work this out. When do you want to come over?"

"How about next week?"

"That sounds perfect."

God, she hated him to the core. But it worked. They'd gotten his attention all right. He sickened her with his talk about caring about "their" daughter. He couldn't care less. She knew he only planned to use them both. She knew his true character. He must think she was actually stupid. But she could use that. So, fine, let him think that. That was a part of the plan too. For now, it was time to go shopping. If she was going to meet the creep in Rio, she was going to go as Charlotte Carrows. Ms. McGee would remain at home. She called her mother to make arrangements.

Chapter 20

One week later, Charlotte Carrows stepped off the plane in Rio de Janeiro and was immediately greeted by a limo driver who escorted her and her bags to the Porto Bay Rio Internacional on Copacabana Beach. She checked into the presidential suite and waited for David.

David planned to use caution. He told Charlotte that he was living in Rio de Janeiro because he didn't want her to know where he really lived. Rio was only 270 miles from São Paulo, and he thought it would be a convenient cover. He rented a car and drove through the hell of São Paulo traffic and eventually into the hell of Rio and its traffic. Charlotte had informed him that she was staying at the Porto Bay on Copacabana Bay, but since he was supposed to be living in Rio, he couldn't check into the same hotel. He booked himself into a modest single room at the JW Marriott, not far from her, and called.

"Did you want to meet me in a restaurant there at your hotel? Or I have some other suggestions for where we could meet."

"Why don't you come to my room where we can have some privacy?"

"That would work," he said, smiling.

"It's room 2020. I'll see you at seven tonight?"

"Sounds good. I'm glad you came, Charlotte. I think we can get through all of this if we just work together. It means a lot to me that you are here."

"I'll see you soon," she said and hung up the phone.

———

Wiping her hands like she had encountered something disgusting, she couldn't wait to get this over with. *Hate, hate, hate him!* She remembered that he said the same damn words to her on the plane while they were flying to Los Angeles to meet her family. Right before he robbed them.

———

David felt in control. He knew he had the power to manage the situation and Charlotte. They'd only been speaking for two weeks, and she was already back to doing exactly what he wanted. She wouldn't be difficult to manipulate. He had the ace of the kid now, too. This was going to be easy. He dressed for her in matching lapis-blue trousers and coat with a blousy white linen shirt. Admiring himself in the mirror and inspecting his impeccable grooming, he would make sure she saw the Patek Phillip watch on his wrist. He reminded himself about how much she had loved him. He would simply make that happen again. Over the years, he'd practiced his skill on many women.

As he walked down the hallway of Charlotte's hotel, he realized that room 2020 was actually the presidential suite. Figured. All that stinking money. Arrogant, stupid Carrows. It wouldn't be long before it was his money, too.

He knocked.

Charlotte opened the door. She was stunning. And different. Granted it had been like four and a half years, but she'd changed. She wasn't the same girl. She didn't resemble the pretty college girl he left behind. She had on a long, flowy red wrap dress with a revealing hi-lo hem. The dress tied in the front under her cinched up and partially exposed bust line. Her dark hair was thickly teased giving her a Katy Perry look with extremely smoked out eyes.

"Come in, David," she said and turned around, barely glancing at him.

He walked into the two-story suite with glass windows and doors that spanned the length of the room overlooking Copacabana Bay. The luxurious suite was exquisite.

"I had them bring a charcuterie tray in case you wanted something to eat. Can I get you a drink?" she said as she rounded to the back of the bar.

"A drink would be nice. Do you have any tequila?" he said as he wandered around the room. He let his hand slide over the grand piano. "Do you play much?"

She glanced over at him while she prepared the drinks. "Not much, but you never know."

He stared at her as she walked up with the drinks in her hands. He noticed the striking invisibly set red ruby and diamond bracelet and the matching earrings. They had to be real. Who was this?

He took the drink from her. "Thank you, Charlotte. It's good to see you again. You look really lovely this evening."

She didn't say anything as she made herself comfortable on the sofa across the room. Drink in hand, legs out and crossed, she looked very confident and relaxed. Not quite what he was expecting.

"Have a seat," she said indicating the sofa across from her. "Let's chat."

"It's been a long time," he said, sitting down carefully.

"Yes, it has. I can do the math too," she said tersely.

"So, you've been in New York all this time? Have you been spending time with your family? All reunited and back together?" he said as he took a small sip from his drink.

"You could say that," she said as she casually glanced down at the Van Cleef ruby and diamond ring on her finger. "We've been close since you left. My mom and I are best friends. She was there for me when Petunia was born. She and my dad visit at least once a month."

"I'm glad to hear that. I'm glad you've resolved your issues and that you have their support," he said as he gestured with his glass to the room. "You could almost say that I helped make that happen."

"You could say that. You look well. Very tanned and fit. It looks like you've done well for yourself, David."

"I have. I'm extremely respected and very much sought after in Rio, São Paulo, Spain, Mexico. I travel quite a bit. Mostly for private museum fundraising and exhibitions. My world is immersed in art just like I always wanted it to be," he said, casually adjusting his cuff, glancing at his watch.

"That's nice. You must be very happy," she said and looked at her glass, swirling the clear liquid, considering.

"I am happy. And what about you? Are you happy? Have you been seeing anyone in New York? Do you still live in the same *tiny* apartment?" he said with a spirited smile.

She downed her drink quickly before responding. "Yup. The same old place. I date from time to time, but there's no one serious. How about you?"

"No one serious for me, either. I don't know why, maybe it's because I travel so much, or I haven't met the right person. Or maybe I just never got over you," he said with a straight smile.

He tried to gauge her reaction and continued. "I've thought about you many, many times, Charlotte. You were my first love. And you know what they say about first loves?"

"That you never get over them?" she finished with a slight smirk.

"That's right! Look at you. You're so beautiful. How could I forget you? It was just such a mixed-up time in my life," he said as he looked down at his hands contemplatively. "I was under so much pressure. I was just a kid, really. Just a kid. I didn't know what I was doing, and I know I made some terrible mistakes, and I know that I hurt you." He looked at her, eyes pleading for compassion.

"You did. Of course you did. You have no idea what I went through. I didn't understand why you left. I never have. You didn't give me the chance to understand what was going on with you. You didn't share any of your pressures with me. If I had known, maybe we wouldn't be here today."

"You're right. Maybe we wouldn't. You and I had a wonderful relationship at one time. I think we could have helped each other. Been more supportive."

"You never gave me the chance."

"That was a mistake. I know that now." He hung his head again and continued. "When I told my parents about Petunia and explained how that could have happened, how she could have been born, and I didn't even know about it until just recently, I had to tell them what I had done to you. How I left you suddenly and that I never reached out. They were ashamed of the way I behaved. And they were right. I behaved badly." He stared at her. "Charlotte, will you ever be able to forgive me?"

She looked at him, her eyes softening with compassion. "Maybe. We have a long way to go."

David, pleased, nodded his thanks and thought that was just fine. He was in.

───────────

David left not long after that. It was almost more than Charlotte could bear, seeing him again. But she had to remember why she was there. God, she groaned, recalling when she saw him shoot his stupid cuffs. Like she was going to be impressed by his watch and success and swoon because he was so awesome. She had to shake it off and get ready for the next step. She reached out to Alex for support. He was waiting anxiously for her call.

───────────

Charlotte and David had arranged to continue their conversation the next morning. They'd planned to meet for breakfast by the pool and then take a walk along the beach. It was another beautiful, eighty-degree day as David looked up and watched Charlotte approaching. She had on a strapless white two-piece swimsuit with a sheer aqua cover-up draped in a toga style. Her ears had delicate, perfectly matched aquamarine drops, she wore aqua-colored Dior sunglasses, and she carried a floppy white hat in her hands. She had the body and posture of a dancer, tall, strong, and toned. She sauntered up to him.

"Good morning, David. I'm starved. Have you ordered yet?"

"No, I was waiting for you," he said as he pulled out her chair. "I did have coffee brought for us."

"Thank you." They ordered an assortment of fruits, cheese, chocolate, and meats, and began to plan the rest of their day.

"I've never been to Rio de Janeiro before. How long did you say you've lived here?" she said as she sipped her coffee.

"It hasn't been too long. A little over a year? I'm renting an apartment in the city, so that should be fairly easy to walk away from when I move back to Manhattan."

"Is that your plan, David? To move back to New York? Where will you live? What about your parents?"

"I haven't worked out any of the details yet. This has all happened so fast," he said, waving his hand toward her. "I think my parents would like to live in Inglewood again once they get their visas approved. They have some family there and lots of friends. The transition would be easier for them that way, I think. I know if I lived in New York it would limit the amount of time I would see them, but at least we would be closer, and flights from LA to New York and vice versa shouldn't be too difficult for us to afford." He smiled at her confidently.

"Are you planning to contact the Met to see if there is something there for you?"

"No, not officially. I think I would like to continue doing what I am best at. Fundraising and supporting exhibitions through the private sector. I've made a name for myself here in Rio, but the art world is such a small community. Moving my base to Manhattan shouldn't be a problem."

Charlotte reached over to the french press and poured herself some more coffee. "One of the qualities that I appreciated about you, David, was that you made your way in the world through your talent and just plain hard work. You're a self-made man. I'm sure your parents are at least proud of that."

"Yes. They have been proud of my success. I appreciate your compliment. My journey from poverty to where I am today has been difficult. But I knew I could accomplish any goal I set my mind to."

Copacabana Beach was a crescent shaped, two and one-half mile long beach. After breakfast, they walked along the beach nicknamed *Princesinha do Mar*, or Princess of the Sea. David went into the details regarding his parents' immigration status and the difficult and painful process they were going through in order to obtain legal status in the United States.

"So, you see, Charlotte. I've come to a time in my life where I need to step up for them and help them complete their journey back home. They're counting on me to do this, and I always intended to. The last nine years they've been in Mexico has been my time to find myself, but now I must be a man and do what is right. The coincidence that I also now have a daughter in the States makes moot any decision I might have made differently. I now find myself in the position to take on the responsibilities and promises I made to my parents and to become a parent as well."

"But, David, you have to understand that Petunia doesn't know you. Our life, the life that I alone built for her and us is safe and predictable. I don't want to disrupt that."

"Life isn't always predictable. She might have to learn that eventually."

"There's something else I haven't told you."

"What is that?" he asked with slight alarm.

"I told her you were dead."

He stopped. Almost shouting, he said, "You did what? You told her I was dead? Why did you do that?"

"Oh, please, David, you know exactly why I would do that. You were gone. You were never coming back, and I would never take you back."

"I understand that you were pissed at me, but to tell our daughter that I was dead was really low of you, Charlotte," he said, his mouth tight with barely suppressed rage.

"She was asking questions, and I wanted her to have a definitive answer that she could accept and she could share if the subject came up at school or with her friends. I didn't want her story to be that her father abandoned her," she said, equaling him with her anger.

He continued walking, trying to cool off.

"This can be fixed," he said with determination. "It has to be fixed. Obviously. Because she is my daughter, and she will be a part of my life. What are you going to do to fix this? What are you planning to say to her?"

"I was hoping I would never have to tell her anything. How about we go back to that plan?" she said, challenging him.

"Look, I know you're angry, but this is not going to go away. I am not going to go away. Ever. Ever again. I won't abandon her. You have my word. You are just going to have to start getting used to it. And I think it would be best if we could work together and not against each other. You'll only cause her pain if she sees you putting obstacles in the way of her long-lost father."

"I don't think I want to talk to you any longer. I'm going back to the hotel. I'll call you later," she said and stormed off.

———————

Vile, evil, man. Hate, hate, hate him! It was "really low" of me to tell Petunia he was dead? He was calling out my behavior as really low? God, the balls on him! She never realized how utterly self-absorbed he was and what a monstrously huge ego he had. But that was okay. She could work with that. She headed back to the hotel to call Alex.

———————

David watched her walk away in a huff. She had a nice way of walking. He enjoyed watching her go. He was pretty pleased with the way things were shaping up. Yeah, she was still angry, but that was okay. She was here in Brazil. She was speaking with him. All progress. He had introduced the subject of living in New York, of being a regular part of Petunia's life, that he was committed to her and would never leave her. She had to believe that, right? I mean, it was her kid. Who would abandon a kid? Even Charlotte probably didn't believe he was capable of it. She would start to accept his commitment to his involvement. She would have to. And once she accepted it as a fact, an unavoidable fact, she would start to negotiate. He was good at negotiations.

———————

That evening they met for dinner. Charlotte had called him and asked him to meet her at the rooftop restaurant at her hotel overlooking the bay. The lights sparkled, and the candlelight flickered all around as David stood by the table as Charlotte approached. Tonight, she had her makeup expertly applied with cat eyes and her hair in a top pony. She wore a bold white trouser suit with no shirt, open to her stomach. Around her neck, she wore a long delicate white gold and diamond necklace and Indian inspired de Grisogona white gold, emerald, and turquoise drops with a matching emerald and turquoise ring.

My god. David realized she had fully embraced the Carrows. "Thank you for seeing me again tonight," he said as she was seated.

"I know we still have unfinished business, David. Whether I want it that way or not," she said flatly.

"Let's get some refreshments and order dinner and take this slowly. Okay? We're here together, that's a good step. How about some martinis to begin?" he said as he signaled the waiter nearby. Maybe that would loosen her up.

"That sounds fine. Good," she said as she smoothed her hand down the front of her suit, not really looking at him.

"Look, I know you're angry at me. You may always be angry with me, I don't know. I've asked for your forgiveness, and I hope you truly consider it. I am deeply ashamed of the way I treated you. I want us to start over. We need to start over now, don't you think? We have to have a fresh start if we're going to have a healthy relationship for Petunia. Don't you think she deserves that?" he pressed.

"I don't know what to think. I'm so upset and confused. You asked me if I could forgive you, and the answer is I don't know if I can. You asked me if Petunia deserves us to be at least civil with each other, and I know the answer to that should be yes."

They paused as the waiter placed the iced glasses in front of them. David watched as she took a large swallow of hers as he sipped.

"I'm really glad you see that," he continued. "I think we can be wonderful partners raising her. I've missed out on so much of her life already. I can't wait to meet her and look into her eyes. It's a miracle that I have a child. I'm so happy that I have her. Please believe me when I say I will never hurt her. You have my word on that, Charlotte," he said gravely.

Charlotte finished her first martini and signaled the waiter for another. She turned her head and gazed out at the bay. "I can't believe this is happening, David. I can't believe I am sitting here with you, having dinner, after all this time." He saw a tear slide down her cheek, which she tried to hide by fussing with her makeup.

Oh, my. That was a good sign. "I know what you mean. I've thought of you so many times and wondered what would have happened with us. It wasn't until I started to grow up a year or so after I left that I realized I had made a terrible mistake. For hurting you the way I did and for leaving you without a proper explanation. But I knew it was too late by then. I knew you would never take me back because I'd behaved so badly toward you. I didn't deserve you."

The waiter brought their drinks. David, still working on his first, watched as Charlotte picked it up and took a large sip. A bit shaky, she said, "I was so alone after you left, David. When I found out I was pregnant, I didn't know what to do! You were gone, and I was carrying your child. I kept hoping you would come back or call or something so

I could understand what happened. It was a very emotional time for me."

"I can't imagine what you went through," he commiserated, "but I didn't know you were pregnant. When did you find out?"

"About a week after you left," she said, closing her eyes.

David took her hand. "Charlotte, please forgive me. Do you think we can ever get past this?"

She opened her eyes and looked down, staring at their hands intertwined, the moonlight shining on them. She lifted her eyes slowly to him and said, "I think I can try."

"Thank you. Now please, tell me everything about Petunia." He smiled at her warmly. "Is she as beautiful as her mother?"

They spent the rest of the evening talking about their daughter. David wanted to know everything about her. From her birth to her first year, her first words, and what she was becoming as she was getting older. He felt they were making wonderful progress.

Hate him, hate him, hate him! She ripped off her jewelry and scrubbed and rubbed her hands and face where she had allowed him to kiss her. She should get an f-ing Oscar. He was actually so narcissistic that he believed she couldn't resist him! What had she ever seen in him? She was ashamed she had ever given him *any* of her time or shed one tear over him. What a waste. She ran to the phone to call Alex. Just the thought of him made her smile return. They were right on schedule.

David suggested they meet early the next day and travel up the mountain of Corcovado to visit the statue of Christ the Redeemer, or in Portuguese, *Christo Redentor*, one of the seven modern wonders of the world. He had a plan.

She met him in the lobby wearing a lightweight nearly sheer silk dress with a floral pattern in green, blue, white, and black with a sequined V neckline. She had on a charming green hat and wore green Dior sunglasses and delicate aquamarine flower earrings.

Brazil's central religion since the sixteenth century had primarily been Roman Catholicism. The ninety-eight-foot tall statue of Christ was built between 1926 and 1931. Designed by a French sculptor, it was built out of reinforced concrete and soapstone, which would show more resistance to extreme weather. There was also a chapel built at the base of the mountain and a rail that gave visitors a twenty-minute ride to the top.

Charlotte and David enjoyed the beautiful journey to the top of the mountain and the cool breeze that came off the Atlantic as they rose. It was breathtaking.

"This is a sacred site for many Brazilians. It's a very busy destination over Christmas and Easter," David said. "We're lucky there are so few people here this morning. Come with me," he said, taking her hand. "Let's have our picture taken over here by this magnificent statue."

A passerby took their picture, and they were looking at it while sitting on a wall overlooking the ocean at the base of the Christ, as David said, "I wanted to bring you here to see this. It is very special to me. Many times over the last years, whenever I visited, and now that I live here, l have come to this holy place to think about my life." He took her hand again. "You have been here with me already many times, Charlotte. I think of you when I am here, and I have asked forgiveness."

She looked away.

"You may think I am being overemotional or even silly, but I wanted to share this with you because it is true. You said that I didn't share enough with you when we were together, that I was too private. And of course, you were right. And we both know where that got us. But I want that to end, now, forever. I want us to leave this place healed, if we can, and start our life together, from this day, as our first day. I promise I will always be honest with you and, of course, I want you to do the same with me."

He took her chin and lifted her face to his. "I know we can conquer anything if we do it together."

She stared back at him and gave him a small smile.

They made the trek back down the mountain and eventually back to her hotel. She had reserved a private bungalow on the rooftop by the pool for the entire day and evening. They lay in it now drinking wine, watching the sun set over the Atlantic.

"I know you told me you can't stay in Rio long," he said, "but I was wondering if I could propose something."

She looked at him, waiting.

"I'm wondering if I could come back with you to visit Petunia. Now that we're healing and getting to know each other better again, I feel so anxious to meet her. I know it's soon, but I really feel it would be a good thing for all of us. What do you think?"

"It is very soon, but I think if you want to travel back with me that would be fine. I've accepted that you want to meet her. I think if we could explain to her together that you are alive, it might be a good thing, too."

And there it was. David felt like he was king of the world. Viola. His magic had worked again. You just had to close the deal quickly. Once they saw Petunia together and were reunited, the real happy family pageant could begin.

"I know you're leaving soon. Do you suppose there's room for me on your flight to New York?"

"Oh, I'm not flying directly to New York. I'm booked on a flight to LA. I'd planned to visit my parents before I headed back home. I have some business there to attend to with Dad, some papers and lawyer stuff about my trust fund or something that I need to take care of. Anyway, I thought since I was traveling, I'd make the trip home."

LA. Did he want to fly to LA with her? If he was going to be a Carrows one day soon, he was going to have to face them again. But he wanted to delay that until he secured Charlotte. She was smiling at him again.

"You know, I actually have business in Los Angeles with the county immigration office that I need to take care of in person. How long were you planning on staying with your parents?"

"Not long. One night. Dad was going to have the lawyer meet us at the house."

"Would you mind if I flew with you to Los Angeles but didn't go with you to your parents' house? I don't think that would be a good idea. I think you need to break it to them gently about me being brought back from the dead," he said sadly but smiled at her too.

"I think you're right. I should tell them about you alone. My flight to LA leaves tomorrow night. I'm taking the red-eye. I'm sure there's room on the flight. And if we travel together, we can spend more time planning how we want to present you to Petunia."

"I just love that you named her after a beautiful flower. I already adore her."

"She's very precious, David. She's my world. I'm sure you'll love her as immediately as I did."

Vile. Awful. Hateful Man. Taking me to the statue of Christ and asking for my forgiveness. And to f-ing say we could get through anything if we did it together. He should keep his precious lines in a ledger so he could keep better score. What a truly evil man. She called the airlines to make the arrangements. She didn't really have a flight booked. That needed to wait until she knew when they were leaving. Together. She also knew that vile David would need time to go back to São Paulo to pack his bags since he didn't really live in Rio. After the airlines, she got on the phone with Alex to make the final arrangements. They were almost home.

David left that evening and drove back to São Paulo to pack his bags and grab his passport. Gullible and predictable Charlotte. Maybe she hadn't changed that much after all. She'd insisted that she make the flight arrangements for him since she had all her travel information. He offered to pay her immediately, but she brushed it off and said they would have time for those details later. He would meet her at the hotel the next day, and they would travel together to the airport and then on to Los Angeles. David really did have business with the immigration authorities, so that was yet another wonderful coincidence that had fallen into his lap. And he wasn't even paying for it. He also assumed their flight accommodations would be in business class. His luck continued to be brilliant! After they got to New York, he expected to be living with them full-time within a month.

Chapter 21

At Whispering Cliffs, Julia Carrows called a meeting with Charles and Henry to tell them she had something vital to discuss. Gathered in Henry's den for the impromptu discussion, the men sat waiting while Julia stood before them.

"Henry, Charles. I want you to sit there while I tell you a story. I don't want to be interrupted until the end. I'm not kidding here. I have something very important, life altering, as a matter of fact, to discuss with you. I've made some arrangements and decisions that will affect all of us, and they are nonnegotiable. I have never in my life demanded something from you. But I am now," she said coldly and clearly as she looked at Henry.

"I have been an excellent wife to you, Henry. I have let you have your way in almost every aspect of our life together, and I have done my very best to support your endeavors and decisions with the proper respect and with a positive attitude. With passive submissiveness, I have let you make decisions that affect us all, and I've sadly come to regret that. I have made some serious mistakes in judgment, as have you." She gave him a hard look.

He sat back in his chair, crossing his legs, and gave her a patient nod to continue. "All right, Julia, I'm listening."

"Our family is broken and I, finally, belatedly discovered that you were not interested in fixing it, so I have taken matters into my own hands. As I said, I have made some decisions."

"Julia," began Henry, but she held up her hand to silence him.

"Not another word, Henry," she said forcefully as he threw his hands to his sides, slightly stunned at her tone.

She continued, "Your daughter Charlotte was exorcised from this family, by you, for the crime of being weak. Weak in your eyes but not in mine. She was born different than our other children. Charles." She nodded at him. "And Carey. That we didn't value her differences, that we didn't embrace them rather than make her feel ashamed of being a dreamer, a loving, sensitive person, and someone whose nature was different than yours was very wrong. You cast her out, and I let you.

"Shame on us both, Henry. But as I said, I have taken steps to set this family back on course.

"I found David Torres. I found the Tsarina's Fancy and its fate. I discovered unequivocally, not that it should come as a surprise to you, that, of course, David Torres alone swapped the Fancy with the paste from the Metropolitan Museum of Art. He worked there and had access to it while preparing the Romanov Jewels exhibit. I hired a private investigator, a Mr. Alexander Macchi, from our firm of Baach, McKenzie & Blake who tracked David Torres's movements to Dubai where David sold the ring and obtained a new identity. Under the new name, David *Cordoza*, he relocated to São Paulo, Brazil, where he is currently employed in the art world and living a very nice life built on our money."

Charles, shocked, quickly looked at his father who looked as confused as he did.

"Mr. Alex Macchi then met with Charlotte in New York and convinced her it was time for her to confront David and deal with Petunia's unfortunate parental issue and convinced her to start living her authentic life as a Carrows. Charlotte, in case you did not see it, attended the Tribeca Ball several weeks ago and announced herself for all the world to be Charlotte *Carrows.*"

She walked over to Henry and handed him her phone, which had a picture of Charlotte in the *New York Post* with her name and caption prominently displayed under it. Charles came over to look.

"She used herself, and in another picture provided to and published by the obliging *New York Post*, a picture of herself and Petunia," she said, nodding at them and flipping her finger, indicating for them to keep scrolling, "as bait to lure David out of hiding so she could entice him to return with her to the United States. She has brilliantly accomplished that. Again, not that you should be surprised."

Henry and Charles stared at her. She walked over and retrieved her phone as she continued. "David Torres Cordoza and our daughter Charlotte will be boarding a plane from Rio to LA tomorrow evening. They will arrive at LAX and be met by Alex Macchi posing as a limousine driver, and by you, Charles." She nodded in his direction. "You will escort David here to Whispering Cliffs for a visit with Henry."

She stopped and defiantly stared at her husband, who had lost some of his steely composure.

"Henry, I expect you will know what to do with him. I ask three things of you. First, please don't kill him. Second, I gave my word that no harm would come to the buyer of the ring, and thirdly and most importantly, I want you to make arrangements that would ensure that David will *never* have the opportunity or inclination to visit Charlotte or Petunia again for the rest of his miserable life.

"Mr. Alexander Macchi will be arriving here in one hour to help make any necessary arrangements. I am leaving, Henry, to get on a plane for New York where I will visit my granddaughter and our daughter, upon her return."

Charles, seeming to recover a little faster than Henry, was smiling broadly at her, thoroughly enjoying her astonishing pronouncements. He was profoundly happy, for a variety of reasons. They all knew he'd find his meeting with David delightfully entertaining.

"Oh, and, Henry," she said with one last icy stare, "if you do not present yourself in New York within one week at our daughter's home, I will leave you. Forever."

At that, she walked out of the room. Henry, mouth slightly ajar, was astonished. Charles, grinning like a kid, supremely happy.

Chapter 22

Charlotte packed her bags and prepared to leave Rio. She put on a comfortable camel-colored Max Mara tailored suit with a white blouse and carried a huge Max Mara bag, which held all her jewelry, money, and passport. She had accomplished what she came to do. She had convinced David to get on a plane with her and fly back to the United States and to Los Angeles. Alex and Charles would be waiting for them at the airport.

David was delighted to be traveling in style back to the United States with a cash cow by his side. He had accomplished what he intended to do by convincing Charlotte, the gullible little fool, that he should be a part of her and their daughter's lives. He was going back to New York as a hit after all.

The nearly thirteen-hour flight to Los Angeles began with a delicious lunch served on exquisite bone china with freshly pressed linen. It was followed by a long discussion and later, a light supper. They slept soundly in their full-length reclining seats and woke refreshed for their arrival in LA at about 3:00 p.m. Pacific Time. They were met at baggage claim by their chauffeur. Since they would be separating, Charlotte insisted they travel together to his hotel in Santa Monica where she'd thoughtfully arranged to have a car waiting for his use. She told him she would then travel on to Whispering Cliffs alone.

The chauffeur loaded their bags onto a trolley and walked ahead of them out of the airport to the curb where a limousine was waiting. The driver opened the back door for Charlotte, who remained by the curb while he and David loaded the bags in the trunk. She pulled out her phone and began texting.

"David, hang on," she said while looking at her phone. "I just need to finish up this text with the babysitter. Would you mind putting a Coke with some ice together for me? I'm so thirsty," she said while typing.

"Sure," he said as he and the driver got into the limo.

After they were both settled inside, Charlotte leaned in the door, looked at David by the bar, and said with an icy-cold voice, "Hey, David, remember this line? Bye, honey, I'll miss you." At that, her brother Charles slid by her and into the backseat. She slammed the door, and Alex took off.

Charlotte smiled with relief and triumph as she watched them drive away and spun around back into the airport to catch her waiting flight to New York.

The door closed on David. Uncomprehending, he looked at the man who had gotten into the limo and realized with a start that it was Charles Carrows. As their driver sharply pulled away from the curb, David had a sickening feeling.

Charles, smiling pleasantly at him said, "Hello, David. It's been a while. Do you remember me?" He cocked his head.

David, his head swimming, realized with alarm that Charlotte must have set this up. That she had not intended to drop him at his hotel and that she was not coming with him. She was nowhere in sight. She had tricked him.

Charles, still smiling stupidly, was waiting, watching David catch up while they rolled out of the airport heading west.

"Where are we going?" David asked.

"Where do you think we're going, David?" Charles said, smiling.

"What do you want?" he said as he gripped the seat, thinking furiously.

"What do you think I want, David?"

"I don't really know. Why don't you let me off, drop me somewhere," he said, looking at the back of the driver's head.

"Where would you like us to drop you, David?" Charles said with a look of mocking satisfaction.

"Just drop me off at my hotel," David said, his mouth pursed with anger.

"Why would I do that?"

"What do you want, Charles?" he said, his voice rising.

"Me?" he said, pointing to his chest. "What do I want?" He expanded his arms wide, looking about him with astonishment. "I'm a man who has it all, David. What could I possibly want?"

"Where are you taking me?" David said, clenching his fists, trying to control his growing anxiety.

"For a ride, for a chat. I thought we'd catch up."

"Okay," he said sarcastically. "What do you want to talk about?"

"What do you want to talk about?"

"Stop that. Let me out of the car," he said as he put his hand on the console and realized there was no unlocking mechanism.

"But we're moving, David, you could be hurt!"

"Stop the car and let me out. Now," he yelled at the driver, who didn't respond.

Charles shook his head and grabbed a glass from the bar, gesturing to David, offering to make him one but then not waiting for a response. He poured a small amount of club soda in a glass and then held it out in front of him, one eye closed, considering it as if it was something foreign. He turned toward the bar and grabbed a bottle of Ketel One and examined it too, then poured three fingers worth into the glass, stirring the contents together with his finger. He licked the liquid off and then added ice cubes to the glass, dropping them slowly, one cube at a time.

David, watching the show, was infuriated now. "You can't hurt me, you know. I'm Petunia's father. You know that, right? Petunia. Your niece? I. Am. Her. Father."

Charles turned on him. "Shut up, you stupid prick. Don't say another god damned word, or I'll end you right here. Are we clear on that? *I will end you.* Petunia's father? You're nothing to me. Nothing to her either, you piece of filth. Let me tell you how this is going to go. You are going to sit there. Over there," he said, pointing, "away from me. Crouch in your corner. Hide from me if you can, you

insignificant spider. I know you're there, but more importantly, whore, understand that I have the power to crush
you. At any moment! And no one will ever find you. No one
will probably even look for you. I know everything there
is to know about you, scum. You're not a man or father.
You're a thief. A repulsive, nasty piece of shit, and I know
how to take care of nasty men. Did Charlotte ever tell you
anything about me? About her older brother? Her family?
You know who we are. Do you think that we got here by
playing by the rules, David? Can you possibly be that
stupid?"

David, his heart racing now, watched as Charles took
a large swallow of his drink and then slammed it down,
splashing some of the contents. Wiping his mouth with the
back of his hand, he then reached into his jacket pocket
and pulled out a gun. A small, but effective looking piece of
steel, it shocked the shit out of David, who reflectively
threw his hands in the air. Charles screamed at him. "You're
a thief, David! And you left my sister pregnant, you fuck-
wad! Did you think you were going to get away with that?"

Charles sat back and placed the weapon across his lap
and reached again for his drink. Sighing deeply, he said,
"God, I hate you, David. Now just keep your stupid, putrid
mouth shut for the rest of the drive. Do as I say and be a
good boy."

David was silent, not quite believing this was happening.
Now terrified, he was trying unsuccessfully not to shake.

Charles smiled at him. Then, leaning forward, he barked,
"Woof! Woof!" and smirked. David watched as he pulled
out his phone and music loudly filled the car. The divider
between the driver had been down the entire ride thus far,
and Charles yelled to him, "Light 'er up there, amigo. Let's

get this package delivered." The panel rose, separating them.

Charles yelled to David over the loud music, "It's the soundtrack from *The Mission*, man. Ennio Morricone, right? Listen to this! 'Gabriel's Oboe.' A fierce-looking king, right?" Charles threw his head back and laughed like a maniac. "Perhaps you'll see one soon!"

David, now gripped in fear, watched his captor sway to the ominous music. With each track Charles grew more animated, shouting out the name of each selection. "'Te Deum Guarani!' 'To God!' 'Refusal!'" Here he wagged his finger in David's face and shook his head, laughing. "'Alone!' *Si*, Davido, *si*." He nodded at him grimly. "'Guarani!'" Charles rolled his thumb and fingers together indicating money. "'The Sword!' 'Miserere!' 'On Earth as It Is in Heaven!' Don't you love it!"

The show went on disturbingly long, Charles chanting along through the choral sections with a wild-eyed look as he pounded along with the tribal drums until the soundtrack changed to Bach, and he mercifully lowered the volume. He said, "I know Yo-Yo Ma. Personal friend of mine. How about you, prick? Ever meet him?"

David didn't bother to respond. He looked out the window as they cruised along the Pacific Coast Highway and knew where they were going. To Whispering Cliffs.

Clearing the gate house and traversing the winding drive, they pulled up to the imposing home. David, remembering his last visit, had forgotten the jolt he had experienced from the grandeur and enormity of the place. It felt more ominous to him now. The driver came to his door and opened it silently. David stepped out, Charles behind him.

Charles slapped him on the back and said, "Move it. Go," and pushed him forward toward the staircase and the front door. They went inside. "Follow me," said Charles as he walked down the hallway in front of him. David had an involuntary moment to inwardly gasp at the wealth surrounding him. The house seemed deserted; the driver remained outside with his bags as the two of them made their way through the cool tiled corridors, breezes pushing at them as they walked through an outside passageway.

David recognized the path toward Henry's office. It was the place where the cabinet containing the ring was housed. Finally, they came to the Moorish arch acting as an ancient reach around the large, heavy wooden door. Charles gave him one backward glance, turned the handle, and walked in.

David followed. He recalled the room almost exactly as it had been so many years ago. It was really two rooms separated by stone columns and Spanish archways. To the right, an office area, desk, chairs, cabinets, and to the left, up several marble stairs, a sitting area, framed by two enormous pastel oil paintings of Charlotte and Carey as young girls in formal gowns. Henry Carrows stood between them, his hands behind his back, waiting.

David looked up the stairs at him and at the older, elegantly suited man sitting comfortably in an end chair, his legs crossed, hands in his lap, a worried look on his face.

Charles pushed David's back up the stairs and then into a chair opposite the older man. Charles took a seat on the sofa next to his father. The two of them stared at David.

The older gentleman cleared his throat and said, "Mr. David Torres Cordoza, my name is Oliver Baach. I am an attorney with Baach, McKenzie & Blake representing the

Carrows family." He looked at Henry who was still staring intently at David and waited.

For some time, no one spoke.

David didn't know what to do, but the awkward silence was killing him. He finally broke it and said, "Mr. Carrows. It's nice to see you again."

Charles threw up his hand in disgust. "See, I told you. He's an idiot. Dad, I can take care of him. We'll just get out of here. You don't have to look at him any longer."

Henry held his hand up to Charles and said to David, "You stole my ring. You were a guest in my home. You were dating my daughter, and you crept in here that night of the party and stole my ring."

It wasn't a question, and David didn't know how to respond. Finally, though, he managed a weak, "I did not."

Charles, again, waved his hand in annoyance but sat back on the sofa, threw back his head, and dropped his jaw in disbelief.

"What did you say?" said Henry in a menacing tone.

David cleared his throat and said, "I did not. What ring?"

Henry looked at Charles and repeated, "He wants to know what ring."

"I told you he was an asshole," said Charles, shaking his head.

"Let's try this again. You stole my ring. The Tsarina's Fancy. We have proof. Not only that, we have a witness."

They sat silent again as David absorbed this latest.

Finally, David said, "What are you talking about, what witness? To what? I don't know what's going on here. He," he said, pointing to Charles, "kidnapped me. I don't have anything to do with whatever it is you think I've done!"

Henry stared hostilely at David while Charles inspected his nails.

"You abandoned my daughter the day after the party," Henry said threateningly.

"We broke up! So what? It happens all the time. We were young, we were dating, it was over. That's all."

"She was pregnant."

"I didn't know that! I swear to god I didn't know that when I left. She never looked me up! She could have found me if she wanted to. She could have told me. She's the one who's to blame for that. Not me."

Charles, looking exhausted, rolled his eyes.

"I want my ring back," said Henry.

"I don't have your ring, Mr. Carrows. I swear to god I don't have it!"

"Because you sold it to Mr. Victor Al Nahyan in Dubai," said Henry.

David, about to protest further, was dumbfounded, suddenly sick that they knew where the ring had gone. They'd tracked it down.

Charles said casually, "When I met with sweet, obliging Victor, he told me all about it, David. He gave you up in a heartbeat. Said he didn't have any idea it was stolen, said you were working on our behalf. You showed him pictures of yourself with Charlotte, Carey, me, Dad, Mom, everyone at the party the night you took it. He told us all about it, jackass."

"I want my ring back," said Henry coldly.

"I don't have it! Ask that Victor person if he has it!" David said, his voice rising in panic.

Charles shook his head. "No can do, David. Afraid Mr. Victor Al Nahyan isn't speaking to anyone about anything anymore. And the ring is gone. Never could lay my hands on it. Sorry, Dad."

David started to shake. Victor was dead? The ring was gone? What the fuck? Had Charles really killed him?

"I want it back," said Henry.

"I don't have it!" David yelled with some hysteria.

"Then you'll pay me for it!" yelled Henry.

"Pay you for it? I don't have that kind of money!"

"Three and a half million dollars. I want it now."

David looked to the lawyer sitting across from him, hoping for something sane, someone who could help, but he was disappointed. Oliver Baach shook his head like he had disappointed him too.

David shook but stood his ground. "I don't have it. Neither the ring nor the money."

"Then we'll take it from you another way," said Charles.

David, his face now drained of color, felt panic; his voice dry, he said, "What are you talking about?"

Henry, gazing at David with hatred, turned to Oliver and nodded.

"Mr. Torres. *Cordoza,* I should say," Oliver said, reaching behind him and retrieving a stack of papers. He placed one on the table and pushed it toward David. "This is a legal document. In it, is a binding Statement of Confession, by you, that you did indeed, take the Tsarina's Fancy out of Henry Carrows's cabinet and replace it with a replica that you obtained while working as an exhibits coordinator at the Metropolitan Museum of Art in New York City. The details of the swap and theft are laid out. Your admission of guilt and the original cost of the ring to Mr. Carrows was $3,500,000.

"The document goes on to say that for the price of $3,500,000 you agree to relinquish all rights, until the end of your life, to your daughter, Petunia Carrows McGee. If for any reason, you break this agreement, you will reimburse Henry Carrows the $3,500,000 forthwith, and he would then be released to take legal action against you."

David was astonished and felt his sweat sickly running down his sides. He looked at the piece of paper in front of him and then into the blank faces of Charles and Henry. He didn't know what to do.

Finally, in a shaking voice, he said, "So if I sign that, you can never call the police, is that right?"

"Ain't no one gonna call the police, boy," said Charles, leaning in to make his point.

"And I don't need to pay you back the money?"

"That's correct," said Oliver. "Once you admit to the theft and agree to the terms."

"And I can just walk out of here?"

"Don't be silly, David," said Charles, slapping him on the back. David flinched.

"We'll take you anywhere you need to go. The driver's waiting out front with your bags. Back to the hotel in Santa Monica? You bet. You're a free man. Take the deal, dumbshit, before we change our minds."

"Mr. Torres Cordoza," said Oliver, holding up his hand and raising more paperwork. "I have some other documents that are pertinent. If you don't admit to the theft and the terms, the following items will also be delivered." Placing the documents on the table, Oliver continued, "This is a letter addressed to the Metropolitan Museum of Art that outlines your illegal activities. There are two others, mostly identical, but personalized to the other two agencies that outlines your crimes. One to a personal friend of mine at the State Department, one to the INS.

"Then there is this letter to your parents, currently residing in Mexico. They are also copied on the letter to the INS that details your crimes, your immoral activities. The robbery, both from the Met and from the home of Mr. Carrows, your abandonment of Charlotte, your name change, your hidden identity. It's all there. I'm confident when I say that the INS, upon receipt of his information would not allow you to become your parents' sponsor for US citizenship."

Oliver waved his hands over the paperwork as he laid it out and finished, "I've summarized, but you're welcome to validate the letters. They will be FedExed in the morning. I'll make a call to the LA District Attorney, another close friend of mine, this evening. He'll most likely need to speak with you too." Oliver sat back, his stare icy now.

"Oh, David," Charles piped in, "a couple other things. One, just so you know we're fair-minded, I've got a small job for you in San Francisco. At a gallery," he said as he tilted his head. "You'll like that right? Get you started back in California so you can get your parents back over here? I also may have a couple of personal things you can help me with in the city too."

David looked at him like he was insane. Charles shook his head. "No? Well, then, one last item of consideration. The Carrows family," he said, pointing to the portraits of Charlotte and Carey above, to his father, and then to his chest, "that's us—oh, and my mother, Julia—we'll make it our personal life's mission to destroy your reputation with every museum, benefactor, and alliance in the art world. Your exclusive little world. We'll crush it. Everything you've built. Everything you are. Gone. For Good.

"So, what say, Davo? Sign the document, and we'll all walk away from this in one piece. If not, well then, that's your choice."

David picked up the paper in front of him, his hand shaking, and looked. Henry reached into his pocket and coolly handed him a pen. David looked at it, instantly recognizing it as a Heaven Gold pen encrusted with diamonds and Tsavorite gemstones, probably worth around a million dollars.

He reached out, took it, and signed.

Chapter 23

Charlotte rode in the back of a cab, exhausted but anxious to get home. She'd spoken with James, explaining that her mother would take over the babysitting and move into her guest room. More importantly, she'd spoken with Pinky and told her to have a wonderful visit with her grandmother and that she'd see her soon.

Looking out the window, the familiar buildings, the streets of New York, the people she loved, she was glad to be back. She wondered how it had gone with David, but she'd know soon enough. What she wanted now, more than anything, was to see her daughter and mother.

So much had happened over the last months of her life. So much had changed. She opened her bag to get money for the driver and stared at another smaller bag that contained all her jewels. Valuable pieces but valuable props as well.

David had been fooled by them and her appearance, thinking wrongly that if she was flaunting her wealth, that meant she was in good graces with her family again. The weird part was that it was true. Not the way he thought, but there had been a change. Thanks to her mom, who'd gone to so much effort to force a reconciliation.

Charlotte teared up. How long had it been since she'd seen her? How long had it been since they held each other? She couldn't imagine what would have to come to pass for a wedge to separate her from Petunia.

But it had happened with her family. And it shouldn't have. She knew why she left, not wanting to be a part of their ways so many years ago, but she knew now that her heart had hardened against them somewhere along the way. Definitely, after they blamed her for the ring and cut her off. But she could have gone to them. The problem, she realized, had been that she wasn't entirely sure if they cared enough about her to make it work. Her mom's recent actions had changed that.

The driver pulled up to her curb. Bagless, since all her clothes were in the back of the limo brought to Whispering Cliffs, she paid the driver and turned her head out the window to look.

Her mother and Pinky were waiting for her, sitting together on her stoop. Gladdened by the sight of it, her heart leapt as she got out, and Petunia ran into her arms. They held one another tight. "Mommy! Mommy! I've missed you! Mommy, Grandma is here! Look! Grandma!"

"I missed you too, baby. It's so good to be home!" she said as she held her. "What have you been up to since I've been gone?" she said as she pulled back to look upon her sweet, smiling, innocent face.

"Well, Grandma and I are playing Stoopy. I was teaching her all about the people-watching game we play. Did you bring me anything from your trip to California?"

"You bet. I tell you what, let's get inside so I can throw off my shoes, and we can visit with Grandma."

Charlotte placed Petunia on the ground and finally turned her attention to her mother. She was staring at them with tears in her eyes. It was a good feeling. Charlotte smiled tenderly at her. "Hi, Mom," she said and walked back into her arms. "Thank you for everything," Charlotte whispered into her ear as they held each other. "I can't tell you how much I've missed you."

Later that evening after Petunia was in bed, the two of them sat down in the parlor to talk.

"God, I'm exhausted," Charlotte said as she dropped onto the sofa and put her feet up.

"It's so good to see you, honey. I'm so glad to be here," her mom said, making herself comfortable in a nearby chair.

Charlotte looked at her mother and wondered about this woman with whom she had had such a complicated relationship. Charlotte hadn't been this hopeful about them in years. It almost felt like she had a new best friend.

"Well, you talked to Daddy. What did he say? I need to know what happened with David, Mom. Tell me everything."

Julia nodded. "You deserve to know. Obviously. And I'll tell you everything he told me," she said as she took a deep breath and began.

"I don't typically like to learn the details about Henry's and your brother's business tactics. But for this one time, I told him that I wanted to know exactly what they did to that vile man."

Julia went into the details.

"You're not saying that someone killed the man who bought the ring from David? Victor?" Charlotte said with alarm.

"Of course not. I was very specific on that point with your father. No one should die, I believe I said. We may have the power to do that, but we're not killers, Charlotte."

"I know that."

"Yes, well, David didn't. So, they let him believe it. I have no moral dilemma with any of it. I think they showed great restraint, and if they had killed Petunia's father, we would have never been able to look her in the eye."

"So, David signed it," said Charlotte with a modicum of disbelief.

"He did. He won't be bothering you or Petunia again. I don't know what Charles did with him when they left, but we can ask him if you're curious."

"Mom, thank you for believing in me and for making this happen. I know you did it all for Pinky and for me, and I know you believed it was important for us as a family. You've really helped. You were really there for me, Mom. For both of us."

Julia nodded her acknowledgment and smiled. "May I ask you a question, Charlotte? Why do you call her Pinky?"

Charlotte stopped and thought about it and then said, "I don't really know. One day I just said it and started calling her that, and it stuck."

"I guess you don't remember, honey. When you were a little girl, I used to call you that. But your father didn't like it. He didn't think it was a dignified nickname, so of course, I stopped."

Charlotte felt something inside of her break. She was moved. And she realized this made sense. She'd loved her parents deeply at one time and the rest of her family too. She was so happy as a child. This childhood nickname came from that time, her time, when they were, in her young mind, a happy family.

Her mother said gently, "I always wanted a daughter named Pinky, but a granddaughter will do." She smiled. "We've missed you, Charlotte. Do you think you could manage a trip or two to Los Angeles with her?"

"Yes, as a matter of fact, I think we'll be out there very soon, Mom. That's another gift you gave me. Alexander Macchi." Charlotte smiled. Her heart was full.

The Carrows adventures continue in:

Titan Takedown
Book Two of the Carrows Chronicles

Available Summer 2018

Acknowledgements

I'd like to thank all the wonderful people of the Minneapolis Western Suburbs Writing Group for their support. The camaraderie, the riveting conversations, and the exhaustive editing were invaluable to me and I feel very grateful to all of you for taking the time to help Charlotte McGee come to life.

I'd also like thank my editor, Erin Liles, whose response to my every anxious e-mail, was always managed with a gracious and patient hand. Thank you, Erin, for your keen eye and professional editing. Thank you too, Manon Lavoie, for your invaluable advice and support in gathering all of the pieces together and orchestrating the final product.

To my friends and family who courageously gave their time and waded through the story, unedited, and managed to come away with enthusiasm for the project, I thank you too. Your support means the world to me.

Biography

Annabelle Lewis lives in Minneapolis with her husband, children and golden retriever. When she isn't writing, she finds time to read. Reading, she believes, has saved her life on more than one occasion.

You can reach Annabelle at:
annabellelewisauthor@gmail.com

Follow Annabelle on Facebook:
www.facebook.com/annabelle.lewis.7967

52533620R00146

Made in the USA
Columbia, SC
10 March 2019